To Marlene and Gordon,

Wish you love
in abundance beyond
all your dreams.

Love,

Aotero

WHAT READERS ARE SAYING

"Entertaining an superful with a touch of eroticism. A page turner."
Nicole Stevens - Bonnaventure, Florida.

"Excellent as a romantic gothic novel. The book holds your interest."
Heidi Gross - Plantation, Florida.

"An intriguing array of events that keeps the reader always
wondering what will happen next.
A literary style that holds your attention and will not let go."
Dr. Nelson Marques, D.D.S.

"Lord Berkely's Wife is an interesting story of sincere friendship.
Highly recommended for leisure reading."
Dr. Yakubu Umar - Assistant Professor of Finance

"Very enjoyable and entertaining. I found the book to be easy reading."
Andrew Nathanson - Software Engineer/Author

"Lord Berkely's Wife is a love story within a love story.
Sotero Agboton has captured the triangle of Benjamin,
Margaret and Jacques with care and precision. The final twist
of fate shows the irony of life's destiny."
Jeanne Jordon - Editor, Sun-Sentinel

LORD BERKELY'S WIFE

COPYRIGHT @ 1994 BY SOTERO AGBOTON

ALL RIGHTS RESERVED

JSA PUBLISHING, INC. P.O. BOX 776 FORT LAUDERDALE,

FLORIDA 33302-0776

TELEPHONE : 1-800-761-1331

LIBRARY OF CONGRESS CATALOG NUMBER 92-090214

ISBN 0-9632616-0-6

FIRST PRINTING : JUNE 1994

PRINTED IN THE UNITED STATES OF AMERICA

FROM SAME AUTHOR :

MISTRESS OF THE FISH TRADING POST,

ISBN 0-9632616-2-2

THE DEATH OF A BATTERED WOMAN,

ISBN 0-9632616-1-4

LORD
BERKLEY'S
WIFE

Chapter

1

ACCRA, GOLD COAST 1952. WEST AFRICA

MARGARET Reevers squirmed as Adjoa, the maid, leaned over the bathtub and scrubbed Margaret's current accumulation of dirt from the young girl's limbs.

Ugh! How dirty you are." Adjoa wrinkled her nose. "Your mama will be unhappy. Do you want that? Sir Reevers will be furious. Do you know that? Come on, wash your face if you don't want to lose your sweetheart, Jacques."

Margaret let herself go limp as Adjoa tried to pull the child upright. "No time for games today. Hold still or I'm gonna give Jacques to another charming girl." Margaret screwed her oval features into those of a clown and stuck her tongue out.

"Tomorrow--while you sleep-- I'm gonna give Jacques to Susie, your friend. Believe me, that's for sure."

Margaret searched Adjoa's face for a sign of forgiveness, but Adjoa frowned and spat into the dirty bath water. Suddenly, the child jumped out of the tub

in tears. She ran toward the door yelling, "Jacques!"
Adjoa stumbled after her little runaway. With her left
arm, she lightly belted Margaret. Off-balance, Margaret
felt her arms and legs flail the air.

Margaret's screams pierced the house, rose on the
wind and burned the ears of Mussa, the cook, the neighbors, and especially Aida, the chief maid, in Henry
Geo's house next door. Henry Geo was Jacques'
father. He had come from Senegal, a French colony, to
work at the Gold Coast Radio Broadcasting's French
service in Accra, the Capital.

Having worked for the Geo family since its arrival,
Aida took a special interest in Margaret.. She trotted
from the Geo kitchen to the fences separating the Geo's
compound from the Reever's. "Hey, Adjoa!" Her
unusually hoarse voice carried even further than
Margaret's. "What you doing to my boy's love? You
treat her bad and I shall break you like a twig."

By now Margaret stood with her nose pressed against
a window watching the uproar. In the backyard putting
charcoal into the coal pot in preparation for grilled
chicken, Mussa glanced up and hurried to the window.
The Reevers' car horn blasted, and the man hastily
retreated to his task. The Reevers stepped from their
car and Aida ran into her master's house.

As Adjoa pulled the pink dress over Margaret's
head, the little girl melted into sobs and convulsive

coughs convincing enough for an Emmy Award.

Mrs. Judith Reevers entered the house, and hands on hips, advanced into Margaret's bedroom. "What's the commotion?"

"Don't you fret. Just my Babyhoney." Adjoa replied nonchalantly, knowing Mrs. Reevers would interpret the nickname Adjoa called the girl only when she was naughty as Margaret whimpering about nothing.

And indeed, Mrs. Reevers turned on her heel and left them.

Mrs. Reevers had nicknamed Margaret "baby" and Sir Reevers called her "honey." Since Adjoa had not known which to choose, she joined them.

Now, as in the past, she crooned, "Babyhoney, Babyhoney," to appease the whimpering child. In addition, Adjoa alleviated the situation by singing and asking Margaret questions. "Who is my Babyhoney? And mommy's baby? And daddy's honey?"

Patting Adjoa's thin arm, then tucking her own arm into the white apron Adjoa wore over her print smock, Margaret hiccuped. " Me, me, me." At first, the "me" came between sobs, then between breaths, then between smiles.

Chapter

2

Sir Reevers was the Governor's first secretary. An eloquent speaker, Reevers was the Crown's spokesman in the British West African colony named Gold Coast.

After World War II, thousands of British Army enlistees came back home. Many families rejoiced their returning whole-limbed sons, some families mourned their dead, and other families sobbed upon greeting their mutilated sons.

These soldiers told of surviving injustices and atrocities, confirming rumors preceding their homecoming. Although these brave men fought a war to free the British in foreign lands, in their motherland they continued suffering under the yoke of those they helped. In total allegiance to the King of England, they shed their blood and lost their lives.

In houses; under shade of trees; in market places; everywhere from neighborhoods to cities and villages across the country, a conscience for change surged. Among the people leaders emerged to guide the struggle from imperialism toward independence, and in spite of governmental threats to imprison or assassinate these men, they increased their political agitation.

In the eyes of Sir Reevers, the Governor sympathized too much with his subjects. On his own initiative, Sir Reevers overrode the Governor and sent anti-independence messages to the Foreign Office in London causing people in high places to hate him. The situation worsened during a reception held at the Governor's palace. Before the committee that drafted the independence charter of Gold Coast, Sir Reevers openly disagreed with the British government's decision to grant independence to its colony. The Governor was outraged. Despite a public apology by the Governor, the guests left singing songs of freedom.

In January 1955, Sir Reevers was recalled to the Foreign Office and forced to submit a letter of apology to the people of Gold Coast and to all members of the self-government drafting committee. Although sad that she had to leave the colony because of her husband's irresponsible behavior, Mrs. Judith Reevers admired her husband's honesty.

Because of the independence issue, the Reevers distanced themselves from the Geos; but their children played together amid news of revolts, kidnappings and assassinations. Things that were natural like listening to the radio became bizarre. People ran to listen to every radio broadcast or rushed to look whenever an ambulance passed. Crowds gathered when security forces inspected houses. These Europeans wearing double-pocket, shoulder strapped shirts with khaki shorts, and above the calf socks, and brown leather boots led squads that crushed any rebellion. They, too, were hated but feared.

January 7 was Jacques' seventh birthday. After receiving an invitation, Margaret sought and was given the consent of her parents to attend the party. Jacques' mother, an active member of Saint Mary's Catholic Church, insisted that the Reevers attend the party but Mrs. Reevers declined. She promised, however, she would send Margaret.

At 9 a.m., Margaret woke up, left her bed and ran to the maid's quarters. "Adjoa, today is Jacques' birthday and I would like to take my bath. Please be fast because I don't want to be late."

"Good morning. Don't you know how to be courteous?"

"Good morning!" Margaret mock-bowed. "Can I have my bath now?"

"Yes, my Babyhoney. One this morning and one at 2.30 p.m. on the dot. If you are late by one second, you will have to stay at home. Today is a big day for your darling Jacques, and you must behave. Go to the bathroom, brush your teeth, take off your clothes, put them in the basket and wait for me in the tub."

On this occasion Margaret became the nicest girl on earth. It took Adjoa only a short time to bathe, dress and give Margaret her breakfast.

"Can I go to Jacques's house now?" Margaret asked.

Local custom decreed that boys and girls be coupled before or after birth according to the traditions of arranged marriage. Such alliances extended to imaginary dimensions, though. Friendly neighbors such as Adjoa and Aida, both maids in their respective households, coupled their proteges.

So Adjoa said, "Not Jacques, but your husband-to-be, your darling, your everything. Now repeat those words."

After Margaret complied, Adjoa added, "OK, but watch your dress and the barbed wire fences if you take the short cut."

#

Dressed in his pajamas, Jacques sat under the oak tree, their favorite playground, eating bread and marmalade and staring at the birds in the sky. Margaret walked to the fence and called his name. She kissed him, adult style, on the lips, and plunked down beside him on the grass.

"Hey, Maggie, my mom has prepared the biggest cake in the world." Jacques held his arms wide.

SOTERO AGBOTON

"Let me see."

"She doesn't want me in the kitchen, and Aida is cleaning the floor in the house."

Margaret stared at his red pajamas. "Why are you not dressed?"

"My mom and Aida are busy. They said that I should wait till 2 o'clock."

"Adjoa says it's 2:30 sharp."

"Well, it's the same," Jacques replied. He was so fidgety that Margaret wondered if he could wait. He rose and tightened the belt of his pajamas. "What were you doing at home?"

"Taking my bath."

"Did you buy me a present?"

She smiled. "Guess."

"I know! Books. Can I see them!"

She shook her head. "My mom hid them in her room. But ... did you read, uh, Ali the Babber and his Cheeses? Or the lad who fell into the lamp? Or the bad sailor?'"

Jacques' round features lit up. "Nope. And I'll read 'em to you when I get through."

"Maybe I'll read them myself, smarty."

"You can't. You're only five. But next year ... Wanna race?"

"Adjoa doesn't want me to dirty these clothes."

While talking, Jacques kneeled down and scrabbling in the earth came across a five-inch nail. He took a stone and hammered it into the oak tree. "I shall put one nail here, one after the other, every birthday, till they reach the highest end of the tree."

Margaret took the stone from him, and hit the nail several times. "When we get married, I shall hit it with you."

Jacques rapidly replied, "But you're leaving this country forever."

Margaret nodded solemnly. "But I shall come for your next birthday party."

"Where would you get the money to buy the plane ticket?"

"My daddy will pay for it." She sensed his disbelief and tried to convince him. "You know I love you and you are my husband, my darling and my everything."

Thinking maybe she wouldn't see Jacques again, Margaret began crying.

At first amused, Jacques became bewildered. So he reached out to comfort her.

"OK, OK, I love you, too. Take this stone and hit my birthday nail."

\#

Thirty children and twelve mothers showed up at the party. The ladies discussed church activities while keeping an eye on their sons and daughters. Every family brought a present. With thirty voices screaming their loudest, Margaret felt as though her ear drums would burst. She put her hands to her ears.

Madam Adediran of Nigeria rose, clapped her hands, requested silence and directed the solemn birthday song. She later introduced games and dances. Margaret felt proud that everyone noticed that she and Jacques were partners.

After many years of training by Adjoa, Margaret danced to African music exceptionally well, but she was singled out also because of her light complexion.

At 7 p.m., the party ended. Margaret stayed after the last party goers left because she lived only a minute away. Jacques' mother went directly to her room to rest. Only Aida stayed to clean up while Jacques and Margaret explored the gifts he received. Adjoa arrived to pick up Margaret who reluctantly followed her. It was an exceptional day for Jacques as well as for Margaret who repeatedly recounted her day to her mother.

The next day after church service, the Reevers bid farewell to the Geo family. In spite of their differing opinions, the women embraced tearfully, and the men shook hands sincerely. Margaret greeted everyone and kissed Jacques in tears. Jacques, disheartened by the separation, bowed his head.

Chapter

3

LONDON 1969.

On a sunny Saturday in July, Margaret and two girlfriends, Betty Hopkins and her sister Michelle, visited Madam Tussaud, the planetarium of historic personalities and crimes. The three young ladies attended the University of London's School of Business Administration.

Although frightened in the chamber of horrors, Margaret felt reassured by the presence of people as they passed through the rooms. The girls yelled and screamed until they moved out into the hall where portraits and sculptures of famous people abounded. Each girl commenting and joking, they snapped photographs of themselves posing with statues of personalities they liked.

Margaret reached out for the arm of an unknown but handsome life-size representation of a man. "Betty, this one, please. He's so elegant, I'll be happy just looking at him the rest of my life."

Easy-going at 24, two years older than Margaret, Betty hoped to get her doctorate in management this year. She wrinkled her nose at Margaret which Margaret took to mean that Betty who had often confessed to having known men since age 16, was not about to let herself be overcome by the allure of any male--real or fake.

Betty's 21-year-old sister, officially engaged to Orville Slaughter last month, snatched the camera and squinted into the lens.

As Margaret stood on tiptoes to kiss the statue, she saw a vein in its neck bulge and its face blush. It was human! The snap of the camera sounded simultaneously with Margaret jumping back. She stammered, "Please, please pardon me. I ... sorry ... a mistake."

His eyes shone with merriment. "Oh?" He took a card from his suit pocket and placed it in her hand. "Benjamin the Unknown, as yet, shall forgive you if your honorable personage will allow his humble waxness to present itself to you in the near future in more human form."

Although rattled by his courtliness, Margaret found herself glancing at his card while replying in kind, "Margaret Reevers thanks you for your courtesy and bids you farewell, good sir."

Margaret clutched the card and hurried to the hall's exit, her heart pounding fast, then faster and faster as her pace increased. Finally giving up all dignity, she ran--blood shutting out all but an indistinguishable blur of voices. She passed the deserting Betty and Michelle and raced three-by-three down the escalator steps to the street. Breathless, she stopped, raised her arms, filled her lungs and turned to face her friends.

The other girls looked away, their wide eyes and loud breathing telling Margaret they had bolted in shock. Margaret giggled at the way their contorted features now seemed more sculpted by hand than the statues they'd admired. She held out her booty:

Benjamin Berkley Lld, Ph.d.
Judge of Courts,
4 U Baker Street, NW1
London, Tel : 631 4831

Instantly, Michelle took a snapshot of Margaret with her battle honor while Betty commented wryly, "And the meek shall inherit what?!"

Margaret hugged the two of them. "I would've run, too, but his eyes ... his eyes froze me!"

As they strolled homeward, Margaret was hard-put to explain to the teasing girls why she had so quickly fallen "under a statue's spell" when "her husband" dwelled in a land far away.

Margaret chided herself for acting so gawky. That was not the image she wished to portray. No, she wanted the outside world to see the 22-year-old svelte, brunette with eyes of Caribbean green that looked out at her from the mirror each morning. Deeply religious, she was saving her body for marriage. She wondered how she could act so strong and dynamic when she talked from behind the podium of the Student Christian Union or before the Saint Augusta Soccer League or the Red Cross but be so shy in person.

Maybe I take on the "air" of my office--the presidency--she thought as she waved goodbye to Betty and Michelle who turned off onto their avenue.

Margaret sighed and tossed a pebble down the street. She knew that inside she wasn't really a volunteer in those organizations. No. Since her parents divorced and her mother returned to London she had forced herself to become involved in enough activities to quell growing resentments. Classes, meetings, studies, and seminars filled every day but Saturday.

Margaret tossed all night long for she had decided to call the "Card Bard," as she dubbed him, the next day. At dawn, she awoke from a dream in which Benjamin was being burned, melted. She saw herself as a child crying and Jacques' arms enfolding her. This childhood memory kept her from going back to sleep.

#

Benjamin woke up at 7 o'clock. He wanted to read documents on three cases he was to preside over but could not concentrate. His thoughts wandered to

Margaret Reevers. Never had he been so eager to receive a phone call. As he looked intently at the phone, it rang once and he answered it.

"Hello, Lord Ben here."

"Could I speak with the Card Bard, please?"

"Only if you'll give him your telephone number, Margaret Reevers!"

She laughed. "I have no cards, sir, you'll have to memorize it: 634-111."

He returned her laugh with a chuckle. "If I retain nothing else, I shall engrave those numbers on my brain."

"Your Card Bard would be delighted if he could spent some time with you. And if you meant what you said to my waxen image at Madam Tussaud's then I am the happiest man in London."

"You cheat, sir! I thought you but a graven image. Still ... I meant every word yesterday. I shall be going to church this morning; afterwards I have a women's charitable association meeting until 5 p.m. We could meet if you wish at the Maestro Cafe, Trafalgar Square."

"Aha. My would-be molester is religious, I see."

Margaret giggled at the image of her grabbing his arm yesterday. "I beg to differ, sir. Faithful is more like it."

"Hmmm. I agree there is certainly a difference. I wish not to intrude so shall we meet at the Maestro's?"

\#

For the first time, Margaret was lost in thought during the meeting. She listened to the presentation of the agenda but made no contribution to its elaboration.

At the end of the meeting, Sister Matilda came forward. "My child, is something wrong?"

"No, Sister Matilda," replied Margaret.

"I am surprised that no word came out of you today."

"But I'm fine, I assure you."

"All right then but I am keeping an eye on you."

Margaret kissed the old nun and left before Sister Matilda could interrogate her further.

Benjamin was ordering his third tea when Margaret arrived. She made herself stroll, restraining the intense desire to run into his arms. Benjamin rose and met her halfway, embraced her and led her to the table. Gallantly, he seated her, touching her hands gently before sitting down across from her. They gazed silently into each other's eyes. Margaret joined her hands together, palm to palm, as if she were praying. Benjamin covered them with his.

Margaret felt theirs was an inward prayer for an everlasting encounter of love. Each sensed a warm and invisible sphere around them. The deep comfortable sensation held back words.

Finally, Benjamin said, "I like your charming eyes and your smile."

Shyly, Margaret responded, "Thank you. My Card Bard speaks beautifully. But is that all he likes of me?"

"I love your hair, your ... your body, your dress, your face--everything."

Everyone's attention was magically directed to them as if drawn by hypnotic rays. Benjamin slowly turned his head, left then right, and looked at everybody but no one in particular to erase the gazes. His gesture wiped away the few glares of those who had forgotten what love is like. Then, he turned to Margaret. "I am sorry, my dear. Please, what can I order for you?"

"Mint tea with sugar. Thanks."

Benjamin raised his arm as the owner approached.

"Yes, Signor, Altieri to serve you." The owner smiled admiringly at Margaret who felt positively beautiful.

"A regular mint tea for the lady please." Benjamin could not take his eyes from Margaret's green ones. Her blouse with its green lace border matched the color of those enchanting eyes.

Some minutes later, Altieri returned with a silver tray. Altieri waved and said in an Italian accent, "Signor, everything is offered by me, on the house as you say. Altieri is not blind. He sees today is a special day." The old man waved away Benjamin's protests.

With reverence, Altieri kissed Margaret's hand. Confused, Benjamin finally conceded the special quality of his first "real" meeting with Margaret and saluted Altieri who returned to his counter. The applause that broke out just then caused both Margaret's and Benjamin's cheeks to glow. They drank, thanked Altieri again and slipped out. Arm in arm, they walked to Benjamin's car. The sun was setting. Here, in speechless consent, they said simultaneously, "No," and turned toward each other in a breathless desire to quench their passion. Their lips touched, grazed and then fed.

Oblivious to passing cars and pedestrians, the couple strolled joyfully, admiring statues, fountains, plants and magnificent buildings lit in the backwash of powerful projectors.

SOTERO AGBOTON

Headlights of automobiles, buses and motorbikes perpetuated the fantasy. Fairy-like crowned ships with a myriad of lights crossed under the bridges and sailed to the South. They walked, revealed their pasts, their dreams and aspirations, made jokes and laughed. They covered an area they had not known before. Suddenly, they realized it was late. The number of cars had gradually decreased.

Benjamin decided to return. On their way back, he said, "Margaret, I want to make you the happiest woman in this world, but you will need patience and courage. I am sure to attain all my goals if God so pleases, but I need your support and faithfulness. It is important to me that any lasting relationship be honest. I shall rely on your word. We have to be honest with each other. Let us share our thoughts and fears, and lean on each other for support. We are, I want to stress this, and must be above all that is material. Nevertheless, I believe we must be generous and open-minded. I want to share your ambitions and help you achieve them. Can you handle that?"

"Sweetheart, I want a man to love, to honor, and to support all my life. Someone for whom everyday can be a fruit of joy and benediction despite illness, sorrow or death. Someone whose anger the moment it flares up, dissipates like vapor, harmless and tranquil. Someone who will still love me as the years pass, as my skin wrinkles, becomes less beautiful, less attractive, damaged by years of sacrifice and devotion. Someone, who, if he still lives, will spare me from a nursing home. I am 22 now, and I believe I can do more things before being introduced to womanhood--if you cannot make this commitment. Can you be that person?"

"If you will marry me?"

"Why not yesterday, Card Bard?! Please, let's talk about it tomorrow. Enough details remain to fill the museum where we met."

When Margaret rang the doorbell and strode in smiling broadly, she saw that her mother had been rereading the note she'd left on the kitchen table. Margaret had deliberately made her message vague having no idea how late or where she would go with Benjamin. She knew her mother worried about her growing independence.

Mrs. Reevers was dressed in a flower print nightgown covered with a Chinese robe in silk embroidered with figures of dragons.

Margaret practically floated over to her, smiling widely. She took her mother's hand and with the other arm held her waist, swung and danced an improvised tango. Mrs. Judith Reevers held her head back and stared deeply into her daughter's eyes. "Who is he?" she finally managed.

"Mom, I am in love; in love with a 32-year-old judge

named Benjamin Berkley. Today is the greatest day of my life. I am deliriously happy and shall marry him this year."

Mrs. Reevers halted and backed away from her daughter's arms. "Baby, did you say ... getting married this year? When did you meet this gentleman? What do you know of him? What about your studies? Why can not you wait?"

Margaret searched her mother's eyes so like hers. "Mom, I love you, too." She cried and rested her head on her mother's shoulder before murmuring, "Don't worry, these are tears of joy. Something you certainly know so well. I would like to take a bath, and sleep in your bed. And please, Mom, have the patience to listen to what I have to say."

Mrs. Reevers hugged her daughter. "Baby, I hope to understand you. Forgive a middle-aged woman's fears. We have all night to discuss things."

After her bath, Margaret came to her mother's room dressed in pajamas. Mrs. Reevers waited patiently until Margaret slipped under the cover. "Let's start from the beginning and try without arguing to use our mutual love and affection to resolve this."

Margaret told her mother how she had met Benjamin Berkley at Madam Tussaud, and about their rendezvous this evening. "Mom, you trusted me all these years, and I hope my responsible behavior proved me trustworthy. I'm not looking for a perfect man, neither am I in a hurry to get married, nor am I willing to fall in love with anybody. I know my friends' experiences have been sobering.

"Mom, I promise to complete my studies, primarily for my sake. A deep instinct convinces me that my judgement is right about my love for Benjamin. I believe he need prove nothing more. At his age he needs stability and love. You know more than I do that ours is more than passion."

Margaret held her mother's face and wiped away the tears. "Perhaps ours is a blind love. If so, let it be one that overflows and sustains duty and sacrifice, and not the contrary. We have no strings on each other-- only mutual love and commitments. Please, please, say yes, and give me this chance."

Chapter

4

Mrs. Reevers listened to Margaret while recalling memories of her own past. When Margaret stopped speaking, Mrs. Reevers rose, sat under the overhead light of her bed, stretched then lowered her arms and fingers. Margaret lay on her stomach, head and chest supported by her elbows.

Mrs. Reevers said, "Let me tell you a story about Judith Shamir before she became Mrs. Reevers, now sitting before her lovely daughter. I was an ambulance driver during World War II when troops of the U.S. and British armies returned from the front. Our ambulances carried many wounded, some mangled badly. During one of those shuttles, I took two young officers about my age. One was your father, shy and timid, the other was an American named Jonathan Jones. He insisted on sitting in front beside me. Jokingly I asked, 'Are you afraid?'

"He replied jovially, 'Life is odd. Hidden danger is always far from obvious danger. Let me see my feet on the ground, dancing, swinging in your arms somewhere in a club, then I shall be happy.'

"Immediately after, he added, 'By the way my name is Jonathan Jones, lieutenant today, general tomorrow.

This is my best friend and savior, lieutenant today, prime minister tomorrow, Sir Antony Reevers.'

"'I am Judith Shamir. Her Majesty's ambulance driver,'" I replied.

"I drove through the dense traffic and arrived finally at the hospital. Jonathan whispered, 'Jonathan and Judith Jones. Three Js. Isn't it wonderful? Please pay us a visit. From my heart, I say don't let me down. Please promise. Thanks.'

"I drove off. I have seen many sympathetic young men but Jonathan was special.

"The next day, I was off duty at 7 p.m. and through your aunt Shirley, peace be unto her soul, by then nurse at the Saint Anthony's hospital, I slipped into the men's ward. Your father and Jonathan were arguing. At first, I heard your father saying to Jonathan, 'You could have held the box five seconds more, and this would not have happened to me.'

"'I'm sorry that I misunderstood your move. I found it easier to throw the box aside than to run to the front of the ship. Besides, we could not hear each other because of the sea and the engine's noise. I am sincerely sorry but grateful to you.'

"Jonathan turned, saw me and walked over. He kissed me. As I greeted your dad, Jonathan pulled me out to the garden. Later, seated on a bench, I questioned him about their argument and he told me how they saved a whole ship. Among their men, they noticed German commandos who had left a box on the deck containing explosives that would have sunk the ship and killed its passengers. Jonathan and your dad were honored for their courage in saving the ship and those aboard. Your dad was wounded but I believe he was jealous that Jonathan received the larger honor.

"Jonathan got out of the hospital two weeks later. I still remember that first day. He bought himself six expensive suits and three pair of shoes. He bought me eight expensive dresses and invited me to a restaurant. We ordered seafood and drank only champagne. We felt so euphoric we could not contain our joy. The war was over and we celebrated victory.

"By three in the morning, we were drunk, but somehow Jonathan was lucid. We took a taxi to a luxurious hotel, walked directly to the bathroom of our room, and vomited, one after the other. As we looked at each other, Jonathan made jokes. I was consumed by his humor.

"Finally he undressed me, left me in my underwear and bra and gave me his shirt. He still wore his T-shirt and pants. He took me to the bed, covered me with the blanket and we slept. The next day when I woke up, Jonathan stood by the bed looking at me. I noticed he had taken a shower.

"'Good morning my princess. I have made sure that breakfast is brought to you, plus four tablets of aspirin, this toothpaste and brush.'

"I sensed my body was almost naked.

"'I have left your majesty in her underwear to prove she was not raped,'" he added.

"I laughed and said, "'You should have.'

"'Seriously, no. Love making should be to the satisfaction of both partners. Love feels better when both bodies are explored--not when one is furtively exploited. I hope I shall have the time and life to share those passionate moments.'

"Changing the subject with his usual humor and imitating the British accent, he asked, "'What does my princess desire beside all these?'

"Amused, I replied, "'To call my sister Lady Shirley Shamir.'

"Shirley was anxious and very angry when I called. You know your aunt and her conservative principles. It is perhaps a reason she never got married. Jonathan asked me for my house address and sent a car full of flowers to my sister. She loved flowers and never received or will receive that many again. Two hours later, we were at home. When she saw me, she cried. Jonathan politely apologized and accepted the blame. When he left, Shirley praised his simplicity and humility.

"The following days, we did not have the chance to see each other as often as we wanted. Sometimes, we met at the hospital. For some reason I learned that Jonathan was confined to the U.S. headquarters because he was in the intelligence service. Then came the day, during a visit at the hospital, when your father gave me a letter from Jonathan in which he said he had to leave immediately for the U.S.A.

"I received two more letters from him through your father. These envelopes I remembered were blank simply because your father tore the original ones and read them. I discovered this recently. Your dad was in the hospital for two more months. I visited him as frequently as I could since he was Jonathan's best friend.

"Later than usual, I visited him one night, and your father was crying uncontrollably. Your grandfather, his only parent, was killed in a plane crash in Australia. I was touched and stayed to comfort him. As a matter of fact, he cried all night. They had planned their future together, and your grandfather was a successful business man. He was in investments. Therefore, your father inherited two mansions, five houses and ten apartments in London, and a large sum of money.

"For a year I heard no news from Jonathan. Your father was my only friend. He took an apartment in town, and got a discharge from active military service. He enrolled at Oxford University to study international law. He encouraged me to take night classes. A year later, he enrolled me at the same university. We saw each other every day, and little by little our relationship slipped into love. It was a steady relationship since we were close enough to know each other. We married a year before graduation. You were born the following year, 1947.

"After graduation, your father, a brilliant scholar, joined the Foreign Office, and as you know, held various positions in different countries. I followed him everywhere, sacrificing my career. Anyway, I was active in charitable institutions and assisted in several related conventions. Besides, I was largely compensated for doing nothing.

"The last country I followed him to was the U.S.A. Then I overheard women talking about your dad secretly dating other women. His irregularities at home became frequent, and indications of infidelity more numerous.

"Once, a waiter in a restaurant where I regularly dined, gave me an envelope. He said that an unknown customer pretended that I had forgotten it on my last visit. The envelope was sealed with my name and address on it. I opened it and found photographs of your father nude with different women. Everything was clear. I kept these photographs believing it was a temporary escapade.

"At the beginning, Jonathan contacted us when we arrived but your father declined all invitations with excuses. Then a year later, the door bell rang. The housekeeper announced Mr. Jonathan Jones. I was reading in the back garden so I invited him to come inside. There he was, with that same infectious smile. The twinkle of his eyes expressed more than the man I remembered. As he sat down and was served champagne, I questioned him. "'Lieutenant yesterday, general today?'

"'No, colonel, precisely retired colonel, and officially as from this day. They say it gives less exposure.'

"We reviewed our past and innocently he asked if I had compiled a book from his letters. I told him that I received only three letters. He was shocked. He had written about sixty letters. I was furious at your dad. Jonathan presented his apology for being less than tactful. He begged me to forget the past but as I briefed him on the photographs, he changed. His apology was sincere but I decided to teach your dad a lesson. Jonathan was very sorry but I did not want to play the victim.

"That evening, your father arrived just in time for supper. He spoke of his day but I was not listening.

Afterward, we left for our chamber. I told him that Jonathan had visited me and told me about the letters. He confessed that he kept the letters for my sake. He said he was trying to protect me from Americans without scruples. I exploded in anger for the first time, for a reason I know was justified.

"'Look, Anthony,'" I said, "'everywhere you served, you tagged people as dictators, alcoholics, drug dealers, communists, womanizers, homosexuals and so on, but you are the most perverted two-legged animal on this earth.'

"I went to the drawer, took the envelope of nude photographs and threw it at his face. I told him that he had better file for divorce in terms suitable for his career. I know that divorce on the grounds of irreconcilable differences seems awkward to you. I knew your resentment but I knew that one day I would tell you the truth.

"A month ago, I called Jonathan and he invited me to his residence in Hawaii. I may be going in six weeks if you approve. Don't say anything yet. It's late now. Let's sleep and think over all these good news. Just know I love you dearly."

"Me, you, too," Margaret whispered, hugging her mother while trying to absorb all she'd heard this night.
    She switched off the light and they slept. As a matter of fact, both knew what to do next.

SOTERO AGBOTON

LORD
BERKLEY'S
WIFE

Chapter

5

Filled with joy, Margaret and her mother woke up with the sensation of closeness and happiness. Margaret turned on the radio while her mother whistled the songs, then they sat on the terrace, and calmly ate breakfast.

In spite of knowing she had a busy day and being uncertain of her schedule, Margaret wanted to see Benjamin so badly she called him.

#

Benjamin was already prepared to leave for his office but instinctively waited, hoping for a call. More than once he walked to the door, hesitant to open it then returned to search for nothing specific. Finally, the phone rang.

"Hello, Card Bard. Margaret would like to know how you are?"

"Very fine, darling. I hesitated calling you to avoid any inconvenience."

"Because of my mother--after I told her, you mean? She could not be more wonderful and is anxious to meet you. Would you join us for dinner this Friday?"

"All the horrors in Madame Tussaud's Museum

could not keep me away. By the way, I suppose we're still meeting today as you promised."

"Certainly, I shall be free at six o'clock. At the Cafe, then? Have a nice day."

"May it rain everywhere but on you, my darling," he replied.

Glancing at her daily diary, Margaret noted Benjamin was the only item besides work. An item both personal and important, she thought holding the small book to her breasts.

Satisfied, Benjamin hung up the phone and rushed to avoid the traffic he hated.

When Margaret left home, Mrs. Judith Shamir remained on the terrace, distantly contemplating the flowers in her backyard garden. A gentle breeze amplified the barking of dogs somewhere in the neighborhood. She reached for the phone and dialed a number in Hawaii. When the call came through, she teased, "Good morning, Lieutenant-colonel ... sorry, Colonel Jones."

"Judith," he shouted from the other end.

"Jonathan, why are you shouting? I can hear you clearly."

"Excuse me. I thought my voice was crossing the Pacific and the Atlantic."

"Oh, Jonathan, when will you change? Not to change the subject, love, but I think I can make it to Hawaii in six weeks."

"Super! That pleases me more than I can say ... but I miss something about London so much that I made a flight reservation for tomorrow. I shall arrive on Wednesday's Pan Am flight."

"Only something about London, huh? You wouldn't be trying to get me out of here? Be honest."

He skirted an answer. Honestly, I will enjoy the pleasure of seeing you again."

"As will I, you. I would be glad to have you for dinner this Friday to meet my daughter's fiance."

"Thanks, Judith, for this honor. But please don't forget to pick me up at the airport with an ambulance."

"Oh, Jonathan, I cannot believe that after all these years you've retained your great sense of humor." They ended their conversation with the customary, "Take good care of yourself."

Even though the University was closed, Margaret went to its library to do research. She later hurried into the students' center to present a letter for a temporary discharge of the presidency to her deputy. Afterwards, she went to the Saint Mary's soccer club and canceled Saturday's trip to Liverpool.

Early in the afternoon, she called her friends Betty and Michelle Hopkins. When she dialed their number, a voice replied gravely, "Hopkins."

"Good afternoon, Michelle. Me, Margaret. You sound tired."

"We were out dancing last night with Orville, and didn't get home until this morning. Betty's washing her face."

"Well, I hoped we could meet in town. I have some especially good news for you."

"Mar, could you come here instead? We could talk over tea or have lunch together. Our folks have the car, and, to tell the truth, we're too tired to take the buses. But please come."

"Sounds good to me. Tell Betty I'll be ringing your doorbell in about an hour."

When Margaret arrived she could not wait for her friends to question her. She plopped down on a sofa, kicked off her heels and raved about her "Card Bard." She watched the reaction on Betty's and Michelle's faces.

For no apparent reason, Betty frowned. She paced the carpeted floor for a moment then sat beside Margaret. "I think, Mar, you've trapped yourself. You're immature for falling in love so quickly. And I, for one, cannot in good conscience attend such a wedding."

Margaret realized her mouth had dropped open and she closed it upon feeling Michelle's hand close over hers on the coffee table. The three sat silently looking at each other until Betty said in an obvious ruse, "Listen, you two, my head's killing me and I'm going to go lie down." She left the room, her brown corduroy pants legs squeaking all the way to her bedroom.

The sound caused Michelle then Margaret to begin giggling. When the door closed behind Betty, Michelle jumped into Margaret's arms. Between giggles, she said, "Congratulations, my friend. You've caught yourself a real beauty--inside as well as outside. What can I do to help make the wedding go smoothly?"

They talked a while, then Margaret arose saying, "I'm meeting my man this evening so I've got to run. Thanks for being a friend."

Michelle went to the door with her and whispered, "Forget old fuddy-duddy. She'll come around."

"I hope so. I miss her already."

As Margaret started her car that early evening, clouds hid the sun and rain poured down. She drove extra carefully. Both she and Benjamin arrived a few minutes late to their rendezvous. Margaret pulled into the parking lot as Benjamin was parking his car. Opening her window, she called, "Ben!"

The rain had slowed to a drizzle and he craned his head out the car window and waved at her. "Darling, could you come here for a moment?"

Afraid that the downpour would begin again, Margaret dashed over.

Benjamin took her hand through the car window. "I would like to invite you to my home if you do not mind. We could drink and discuss in privacy." He kissed the back of her hand.

Nodding, Margaret got into the car and kissed him. "You always have good ideas."

Margaret felt a bit cold in her damp dress so Benjamin turned on the heater and wrapped his arm around her shoulder. He pulled her closer to him and kissed her while cautiously driving with the other hand. She leaned against him and asked about his day.

"You know, Darling, I'm in a very sensitive area of the judicial system. Takes a lot out of me. Every case is different. Whatever one's experience, making some decisions is tough and one must use human reasoning to interpret the law. I must judge a person's action in relation to the law, the law of men, laws enacted before I was born. Although I don't argue over their legitimacy, I sometimes feel that our decisions from the interpretation are wrong with respect to the spirit of those who enacted them." He sighed. "I don't know if you understand what I mean."

Margaret nodded. "When you talk about people and the law, it sounds interesting. Please tell me more."

"You know, Darling, every decision a judge makes is delicate. In this arena where the prosecution, the defense, the public and more often the media are very good actors, we alone make the decisions. We always say that we judge to our best convictions, but we are poor and very often helpless. Sometimes I wish I had a mystical power to know the truth. When I began my career, I wanted justice for all and pushed my ideas. But in our complex system, I have many times lost the meaning of justice.

"You will have to become acquainted with my life of discretion, silence and absence of mind. For the latter, I beg for your lenience and patience." He pulled into a driveway. Well, here we are. Hey, how come I have monopolized the conversation during our journey? What potion do you have?"

"Darling, you needed to talk to someone and I loved listening. And have I told you I not only love you but that I also like you?"

Benjamin kissed her long and deeply. A moment later he opened the house door and stood aside to let Margaret enter. She looked about intently. The interior was completely white. The principal hall consisted of a large room partitioned into two compartments. One was a fully equipped kitchen--also painted white.

Green house plants and cut flowers were tastefully arranged, their fragrance contributing to a peaceful atmosphere. The furniture was in natural varnished rattan, the cushions fashioned of cotton material in various floral designs. Not only is the house luxurious, it is also clean, Margaret thought. "Is this paradise?"

"To me. The architect based the designs on my ideas. This place is my refuge. May I serve you something?"

"A Martini, please."
Going to a bar also of rattan, Benjamin made them both Martinis which he brought back on a tray and placed on the table in front of the sofa where Margaret sat, shoes off, legs pulled up under her.

Sitting as close to her as possible, Benjamin said, "When the weight of emotions and sometimes loneliness overwhelms me, I sit here and sing or pray. Nothing beats those refreshing times."

"Do you really pray?"

He took a sip before answering quietly. "Oh yes, above is a God that answers and overshadows all turmoil with love. I speak out of experience."

Margaret touched his hand. "I believe you. I just realized how much I want to learn about you."

"I, too, am eager to know my intelligent fiance better." Benjamin reached out and kissed her.

Margaret responded passionately, her heart racing. She felt her face flame with the blood rushing to her head and her stomach cramp in delicious throbs. She closed her eyes as the warm hands of Benjamin explored her body causing sensations from her scalp to her loins. She whispered, "Ben, it's going to be the first time. I mean that I am a virgin."

She looked up at Benjamin and thought he looked surprised.

"Love, you have my admiration and respect. But we must talk over this subject. I shall stick to your choice; sex before or after marriage. Even though I may be hurt, I shall content myself if you choose a platonic relation."

She whispered, "Honey, I love and respect you,

also. I am not conservative but I want to honor the man I love. I will concede if this should cause a conflict. You deserve the honor of your life companion and I wish to be that person."

Benjamin was touched by Margaret's speech. He knew the profound meaning of these values which he had many times ignored. Gently he lifted Margaret from the sofa and sat her on his lap. "I love you, Sweetheart."

Margaret faced him, kissed his cheeks and lips, and felt thankful for his elegant attitude. More than ever, she wanted him. Tired, they sat face to face, eyes to eyes, drawn in admiration.

Doubts assailed Margaret. "Are you certain you're ready to settle down? I mean, are you stable? I know you've been a bachelor a long time. Can you cope with someone living with you? Please don't rush into a commitment with me because when I marry, it will be forever. I'm patient enough to wait."

"Darling, I know we can make it. But we must trust ourselves, let love be our strength."

Once again they kissed and Margaret felt her passion unendurable. She moaned and when Benjamin looked into her eyes, she nodded.

She felt Benjamin lift her and she hugged him tightly.

In the large bedroom, she moved only when necessary as Benjamin slowly undressed her. She watched as he--his eyes remaining on hers--removed his coat, tie and shirt. Then he knelt on the bed beside her and they kissed, falling together against the pillows. Benjamin's body released warmth that gave Margaret thrilling sensations all over, from the tips of her finger nails to the roots of her hair.

Margaret responded with fierce wet kisses and cooing. Gently, Benjamin's tongue slowly explored her ear, neck and breast. Each lick from him caused tiny tingling shock waves.

Margaret felt him pull away and looking up saw him strip off his trousers and underpants. Then he lay down upon her. Below her abdomen, the circular massage of his pubic hair against hers excited her. As he pressed more and more, he provoked in Margaret a thrusting release into ecstasy. This discharge echoed in Margaret like the sound of a cymbal with diminishing waves.

Although he had not penetrated her, to Margaret, the foreplay was an intense and joyful discovery and to Benjamin, it confirmed years of experience. Benjamin was satisfied. After savoring a moment of silence, Margaret caressed Benjamin's head. Benjamin kissed her.

"You are my life."

They talked for long moments and then fell silent,

satiated. After awhile Margaret glanced at her watch. It was 9:15 p.m. She looked at Benjamin whose eyes were closed, and asked, "Honey, are you sleeping?"

"Just enjoying this moment, wishing it might never end."

Margaret passionately kissed him. "I love you and wish to stay but ... May I use your bathroom please?"

He gestured across the room. "Certainly."

Stepping into the bathroom, she stopped in surprise at its beauty parlor decor. The walls were entirely mirrored. Four brands of men's products, each a complete line, were arranged on glass shelves.

As though reading her thoughts, Benjamin called, "Darling, just fancy what I dream for you if I love myself this way."

Margaret laughed. "Thanks. In advance."

Ten minutes later, she came out dressed and more beautiful than ever. Benjamin was dressed and drinking a dry gin. He seemed fascinated. "Margaret, you are the most beautiful woman I know. I can't afford to lose you."

"Thank you, my lordship. And your lady thinks you are a wonderful person. She is yours, forever."

"I know I asked you before but you just said, 'Let's talk later.' Now I'm asking again. Will you please marry me?"

"Is this a serious proposal?"

"If you agree, my love. I intend to request your hand of your mother, this Friday." He cocked an eyebrow and waited.

"Yes. Ben, you can't imagine how happy I am." Margaret emptied her glass and rose to leave, but Benjamin pulled her and lavishly kissed her. Again, and again. She laughed and asked, "Darling, when will I get home?"

"How does next month sound?"

They were both laughing as he opened the door and escorted her out.

After leading her down the steps, he opened the car door, closed it and walked to the trunk. He opened it and brought a bouquet of flowers to Margaret. Touched, she could not stop tears from pouring down her cheeks. "Thank you. I love you." She kissed him.

Benjamin pulled a handkerchief out of his pocket and wiped her tears. He drove her home while they talked of clothing, food, cars, politics, marriage, children and their other dreams. Margaret had the ability to bring up subjects and to listen. Benjamin was intelligent, mature and convincing. Both had similar ideas and were skilled communicators.

When the car stopped, Margaret said, "I would love to see you tomorrow."

"We can see each other every day if you want, and I shall be with you every hour you want. By the way, I would like you to be my date at a reception this Wednesday. Can you make it?"

"I'd be delighted, Ben." She kissed him and whispered, "Until tomorrow." As she unlocked the front door and stepped inside, she noted that Benjamin waited until she entered the house before driving away.

Chapter

6

The following day Margaret and Benjamin went to a concert staged by Brazilian musicians which they both enjoyed immensely. Benjamin assessed Margaret's dancing abilities at far above his. In fact, she danced so well that he was intimidated. For every step he initiated, Margaret responded in synchrony, and even tried variances. Very often, she led. Because of this magical quality in her body that belied her humble manner, Benjamin wondered if she were a professional dancer.

On Wednesday, Benjamin and Margaret appeared at the reception. The couple was sensational. The host, Fred Timer, President of the International Investment bank, seemed taken by Margaret's beauty. Although He was Benjamin's closest friend, Fred knew little of Ben's private life. Over the years, various rumors circulated that Benjamin had feminine tendencies. This day, however, the 250 guests watching the couple discounted the rumors. Eyes could not stop following as Margaret and Benjamin danced.

Teasing, Fred came by and said, "Hey Ben, I am the host yet you two are the stars."

"Then how about paying us for the entertainment?" Benjamin replied and they laughed.

From waltz to bolero, cha-cha to rhumba, Margaret and Benjamin danced. By 2 o'clock in the morning, Benjamin was tired. Margaret laughed.

"I'm very tired, also, but I enjoyed my secret challenge to see who would last the longest. I win."

They thanked Fred and walked to Benjamin's car where Margaret said, "I am coming to your house tonight."

.

In the process of scrabbling in his pocket for car keys, Benjamin stopped short. "I'm pleased you want to."

Margaret pushed against him and leaned her head on his shoulder. "Ben, thank you for this wonderful evening. I'm so happy to be by your side. I love you."

"I love you too, Honey. You were marvelous tonight--even Fred was jealous."

Once in Benjamin's apartment, they kissed and hummed as each tasted the salt of the sweat on the other's slick necks.

"Let's bathe together," Benjamin suggested. Hand in hand, they undressed in the bedroom then kissing, moved to the bathroom. Benjamin opened the taps to control the water's temperature. Making certain the water felt just right, he helped Margaret into the spa. They sat close to each other, lips joined, warm tongues fused.

Margaret caressed his thighs then moved to his erect penis while the warm water rose above their waists. Her fingers, in a loose grip, massaged his organ.

After all his sexual exploits, Benjamin was amazed to feel new sensations in his abdomen. He drained most of the water from the tub while moving his hand slowly over Margaret's flanks. She made a soft whining moan. Slowly he kissed her and positioned his head between her thighs with his face brushing her pubic hair. For minutes, Margaret convulsed and groaned until she reached orgasm.

Letting the tub fill again, Margaret dipped herself in the water while Benjamin rose and sat on the edge of the tub with his legs spread. Margaret washed his penis and put it in her mouth. She sucked it and lubricated it with saliva. Benjamin held her head down on it several times as the muscle of his butt tightened. Soon, spasm after spasm, he ejaculated.

They rinsed, dried off and covered themselves with towels. They kissed and danced into the bedroom where Margaret, partly apprehensive, partly imploring, whispered, "Benjamin, please let's wait a bit. I'm not ready now. Please understand me."

"Not to worry, my dear, I'll wait until you're ready."

Margaret hugged him, afraid that by putting him off she might lose him. Instead, he calmed her and lay by her side on the bed. Yawning deeply several times, they slept.

The next morning when Margaret woke up, Benjamin had gone to work. He had prepared breakfast and left a note on the tray. "Good morning, Honey. I shall be back by 5:30. Here's a spare key for the door if you should leave before my arrival. With love, Ben."

Margaret showered, ate breakfast, dropped the dishes in the washer, and left for home. The house was empty when she arrived. Probably, Mom is still with her friend, Mr. Jonathan Jones, Margaret thought.

Margaret called Sister Matilda to excuse her absence. Sister Matilda guessed the reason immediately. "Are you in love?"

"Yes, but let's keep it a secret until I can announce it myself."

"My child, I promise. God bless you and the unknown man."

"His name is Benjamin Berkley. Good-bye, Sister Matilda."

SOTERO AGBOTON

Margaret's mother arrived later. She walked to her daughter's room and opened the door. Margaret called to her. "Mom, come here."

"Baby, what's wrong?"

"Just tell me, have you been drinking?"

"Only champagne. And I had a wonderful night. I suppose yours was, too?"

"Very. We are getting married in four months. Benjamin wants to announce it tomorrow."

"Baby, Jonathan also asked me to marry him, and I have replied positively."

"Are you in love?" Margaret asked.

"Yes, just as you are. Jonathan is the man I've dreamed of. He is positive in every way. Oh yeah, life is experience or vice versa. Well, I'm tired and don't know if I'm making sense."

"Come on, Mom, you do. Do you want anything."

"No, thanks, I'm going to bed right away. Wake me up for supper."

During supper, Margaret and her mother planned

what they would serve for Friday's dinner. Both women were excited. Mrs. Judith Shamir decided to use two bottles of wine from her cellar; Bordeaux Dom Perignon and a Laurent Perrier Champagne. After all, she thought, my guests are more than honorable.

Margaret reached for her mother's hands. "I thank you for everything, Mom."

Chapter
7

The next morning, the door bell rang. Mrs. Shamir opened it. "Good morning. I am supposed to deliver these flowers to Mrs. Judith Jones," the delivery man said.

"Oh, I'm Judith Shamir--soon to be Mrs. Jones." She laughed and gave him a tip. She opened the envelope and read the note.

"My gratitude to you, lady of my life. Je t' embrasse. I love you."
Jonathan

Mrs. Shamir gazed at the dozen majestic gladioluses, skillfully arranged within a purple ribbon. She put the flowers in a vase that she centered on the living room table. Again the door bell rang. A boy in a red cap, red coat, white gloves and black pants said, "Good morning, Madam, this bouquet is for Miss Margaret Reever."

"Good morning, Sir, I am her mother and shall give it to her. Thank you and goodbye."

Margaret was talking on the telephone with Benjamin when her mother knocked at the door with the flowers. Inquisitive, Margaret looked at Mrs. Shamir as she handed the envelope to her. Margaret unsealed it. "Good morning. With love from Benjamin," she read.

"Oh, what a surprise, Darling! Thank you dearly," she said into the receiver.

A few minutes later, Margaret exited her room to see more flowers. Their abundance created an atmosphere that motivated both women to start the preparation for the evening's dinner. They wanted it to be successful and entertaining. During the day, they shared suggestions and executed their tasks with zeal.

Late in the afternoon, rain poured, and Margaret cursed as she looked through the window. "Wasn't it enough that you had to drizzle?" she complained. Her mother came to her and patted her shoulder. "Calm down. It's going to be a nice evening, even if it snows."

"Softly, Margaret replied, "Mom, you know a day without rain would be perfect."

Mrs. Judith Shamir did not want to argue, and finally whispered, "That's the difference between London and ... Honolulu."

At 6 p.m., all was ready and the women went to get dressed. An experienced hostess, Mrs. Shamir knew what to wear. Margaret came to her room from time to time to seek advice on such and such combination of outfits.

At 8 p.m., the door bell rang. Mrs. Shamir opened the door. Jonathan stood in the doorway holding out a bottle of champagne in one hand and a bouquet in the other. "How beautiful you are, Judith. You are a star."

She closed the door and kissed him, a gentle and soft welcome. She took the flowers and led him to the living room.

"My daughter is getting dressed, and we are expecting her fiance." Looking into his eyes, she continued, "Thanks for all these flowers. You are lovely, and don't argue with me."

"I shan't, then!" Jonathan said.

"What may I serve you?"

"A cognac, please."

The bell rang once more and this time, Margaret went to open the door. Benjamin was dressed in a black suit, a white shirt with a bow tie. Margaret invited him in.

"Good evening, Honey. You are the most beautiful woman I've ever seen." He handed her a packet.

"And you are the most elegant gentleman," she said and touched his lips. "Thanks for the flowers. My mother and her friend Mr. Jonathan Jones are waiting for us."

She looked down at the package she held. "Swiss Lindt chocolates! I love them. Thanks."

They entered the living room, where Margaret began the introductions and her mother finished them.

After everyone sat, Judith asked with a twinkle in her eyes, "What can I serve to your honor?"

Benjamin grasped the allusion. "A cognac. Thank you."

"That is shorter than a sentence," added Jonathan and they laughed.

The bit of repartee broke the ice, creating a friendly atmosphere. Benjamin and Margaret immediately liked Jonathan because his sparkling eyes and his twitching lips told them he was a cheerful person. Margaret was happy to see that his humor touched everyone. Although serious at the beginning, the discussions were filled with jokes and stories.

Jonathan was facile in that manner. He spoke in a low tone but his gestures made figurative images of everything. His ability to imitate people in different languages added realism to his stories. His ability to maintain the pleasure was incredible to Margaret. He took the conversation at one point then gave it at another with tact and intelligence. By the time dessert was over, Margaret noticed it was midnight.

Finally, Benjamin, serious, rose and formally asked for Margaret's hand. He held her hand and after Mrs. Shamir's approval, slipped an eighteen-carat gold ring garnished by three diamond stones around her finger. Margaret kissed him while Judith and Jonathan applauded.

Happily, Benjamin and Margaret turned to them. "Mrs. Shamir, I thank you for this wonderful dinner and evening. Mr. Jones, please accept my gratitude. With your permission, I shall have to leave. I wish you good night."

Margaret wanted to spend some time with Benjamin alone. "Mom, I shall leave with Ben. Mr. Jones, it was a delight meeting you. Thanks for this great evening."

Jonathan replied, "My pleasure. So long."

Judith bid Margaret and Benjamin farewell and closed the door. When she returned to the living room, Jonathan was standing. Drawing from his vest a box, he removed a gold ring with sixteen diamond stones. He took her hand and said, " My dear Judith, will you be my wife?"

Trembling with joy and in tears, she replied, "Yes." They kissed then she said, "Please take me to my bedroom, first door after the stairs."

In the bedroom, Jonathan lifted Judith as she untied and removed his shirt. He lay her down on the bed and closed the door behind them. They undressed and slipped under the sheets where their warm bodies met in a prelude to a gentle battle of desire and passion, masterfully enriched by experience. Not until 3 o'clock in the morning did the heat of their fire die down. Tired, they slept side by side, hand in hand.

Margaret and Benjamin drove directly to his house while Ben recounted anecdotes from the evening with her mother and Jonathan. She leaned on Benjamin as he spoke. His nearness kindled the desire to have him all to herself, so she reached out for his lips. From the car, up the stairs, to the house, Benjamin responded passionately. Margaret looked at him with insistence and said, "I would like it to be today."

Hesitant, Benjamin pressed her against his body while each kiss increased his desire for her. He led her to the bedroom. Slowly, he undressed her and revealed her nudity. Margaret helped him remove his shoes, socks, and trousers before she lay on him. Benjamin reached out for the bedside lamp and reduced its beam.

Margaret boldly explored his chest, stomach and penis. She moaned as the aura caused by the gentle scent of an eau de cologne on Benjamin's body overwhelmed her. Benjamin took the initiative, caressed and

massaged her clitoris until her vagina got wet. He penetrated her, at first shallowly, then deeply. He stroked
fast in and out so that she sensed a pain followed by an
immediate pleasure. Margaret wanted more until she
reached orgasm. When she paused, he moved off her.

Benjamin rose from the bed, walked to the bathroom, turned on the taps, poured in soap and returned
to the bedroom. He approached Margaret and asked,
"How are you feeling, Honey?"

"Just too wonderful. I am in a dreamland. I thought
the first time would be traumatic but -- Oh! You are
even more wonderful than I knew. I love you, Ben."

"I love you, my queen. Come, I have prepared a
bath for you." Benjamin carried Margaret to the bathroom and dipped her into the warm foamy water. Then
he helped her wash off the few drops of blood. Margaret caught him with one arm and kissed him. "Ben, I
want you even more. It's perhaps going to be every
day."

"My love, you have all your life to prove it.
Remember I care for and want to share everything in
your life."

"Ben, I want you."

Wrapping her in his embrace, Benjamin led her to
the bed, and once more they made love. Afterwards,

exhausted, Margaret closed her eyes. Benjamin looked at her serene and angelic face as she slept. He kissed her forehead and switched off the light. This time he had found the woman of his life.

The next day, Margaret called her mother and told her that she was going to pick up some clothes and spend the weekend with Benjamin. They planned to go on a picnic.

Margaret watched the sun rise in the sky and thought what a beautiful day for their outing. Listening to Benjamin in the shower, she sang along with him as she prepared breakfast which she served in the kitchen. Dressed in linen pants and a polo shirt, Benjamin pulled her chair out before seating himself. "You have good taste in clothing, my Card Bard."

"I choose to live well, my darling, but not so well that I get in debt."

They drove to the woods and spent a loving day on the shore of a river.

The following weeks after this wonderful weekend were busy ones for Margaret. After office hours, Benjamin helped her make the guest lists. Margaret named 30 guests and Benjamin more than 200. He did not want to offend any of his friends, and rationalized that for the past ten years he had been invited at least once a week to various ceremonies.

SOTERO AGBOTON

Of the 500 friends scattered around the world in his address book, he had been able to keep contact with nearly all, at least once a year. Because of the number of guests, he called a contractor to organize the wedding. He confided his plans to Fred Timer who volunteered to handle the music.

Chapter

8

One morning Benjamin looked out at the land-scape from the bedroom window.

A young cock jumped to the top of an empty barrel, looked over the barn, flapped its wings, puffed out its chest like a drill-sergeant, and crowed. Proudly and majestically, it descended while gripping a piece of leaning wood.

Coming up behind Benjamin, Margaret held his waist and nodded toward the rooster. "That looks like you, my love."

Benjamin grimaced then smiled. "I suppose I am telling the world of my wedding, my love and my life." Turning, he gave her a hug, then lifted her and walked to the bathroom.

Benjamin and Margaret decided to celebrate their wedding party in his parents house thirty minutes from the city. The house contained eight bedrooms, a great guest hall, and three independent living rooms. A luxu-riant garden surrounded the estate. The Berkleys, both retired medical practitioners, had lived for the past five years in Sydney, Australia. They took a flight home the night before the wedding, and after a family dinner, retreated to the right wing of the house.

Judith Shamir refused the offer to spend the night in one of the visitors' apartments. With Jonathan, she promised to return the next day before noon. Jonathan's presence assured Benjamin that Judith would not worry too much over losing her only daughter to another family. The long hug Margaret and Judith shared further reassured him.

The morning of the wedding, Margaret and Benjamin went to the kitchen for breakfast. Margaret was surprised to see a man supervising drinks and food and speaking French and English.

"Yes, ici, Par la, please." The man turned his head. "Good morning, Ben."

Benjamin introduced him to Margaret. "Margaret, this is my friend Serge, Chef at the Hilton Hotel. He is the contractor who is supervising the catering service with Altieri of the Maestro Cafe."

"Good morning, Serge," she said and added in pleased surprise, "I did not know you invited Altieri."

"Yes, he did," Serge said.

"Yes, he did," repeated another voice from the door behind them. "And I am honored, my lady. Good, good morning, lady and gentlemen," he said in an Italian accent as he strode through the doorway. "For the first time in twenty years, I am called to serve a British wedding. I swear that I, Pepe, will make yours a day of everlasting remembrance." A short good-looking woman followed him. "This is my wife, Margarita."

Holding out a paper to Serge, Altieri added, "Mr. Serge, your invoice with the corresponding drinks. Notice I have attached items my wife and I delight in giving as gifts for the wedding. In my country, the whole village knew of my wedding. Today, this city will hear of my friend's marriage. I, Pepe, swear this."

After the greetings, Benjamin intervened and thanked Pepe. "Pepe, you and Serge must make this day a fiesta."

When Benjamin pulled Margaret out of the kitchen, Serge followed them. "Ben, we have so far used about half the budget. I have fifteen lambs barbecued. We are taking a Moroccan dish called couscous with raisins and olives. We have fifteen cases of champagne and many other drinks besides those brought by Signor Altieri."

"Thank you, Serge, for everything. Take whatever initiative you feel suitable. See you soon." Benjamin held Margaret's hand and crossed the guest hall to the terrace.

Fred Timer with three other men were installing the

sound system. They waved at Benjamin and Margaret when he whistled to them. Hand-in-hand with Margaret, Benjamin turned and moved to the right wing of the house, to his parents' quarters.

Benjamin knocked lightly and Mrs. Berkley opened the door. "Good morning, my children."

She kissed Benjamin, then Margaret. Mrs. Berkley laced an arm around Margaret's waist. "Come see your father-in-law. Can you believe the old man still believes he is a bull?"

Dr. Berkley was doing pushups and sweating profusely. Upon spotting the women walking toward him, smiling, he said to Margaret. "Hi, Honey, you better keep that husband of yours in good shape. Six years ago, he won a wrestling competition against me due to the arbitrary decision of his mother."

Amused, Benjamin stood at a distance to avoid his father. "Over here, Son. I shall wait until next year for revenge--only because today is your wedding day. Have some coffee."

Dr. Berkley looked over his shoulder at Margaret and shrugged as if to say "Do you see this coward?" He took a towel, wiped himself and bustled over to kiss Margaret's hand. "I apologize for the perspiration, but it is very clean."

They laughed and sat for coffee. After a moment,

Benjamin broke the silence. "Dad, we plan to stay all day and night so long as the festivities go on. We don't intend to skip off as is customary. Our departure to Venice will not be before tomorrow evening. In any case, we'll leave with you to the airport."

Mrs. Berkley spoke up before her husband could. "I think the idea is superb. It is your day, so enjoy it the way you want. Benjamin, the men will be using the right wing of the house, and we intend to use the left one."

To Margaret she said, "Baby, you've only an hour left before you start dressing. Your mother should be here in a short time for the preparation. And Son, I invited Dr. Scott to the wedding--in case of an emergency."

"Good, Mom," replied Benjamin and taking Margaret's hand he rose to leave.

Dr. Berkley led them to the door where he slipped something into Benjamin's hand. He made the transaction so quickly that the women did not notice it. They laughed at his funny gesture but only Benjamin understood his father's sign.

Benjamin and Margaret climbed the stairs to their room and lay on the bed while he unfolded the paper in his hand. It was a 900,000 Sterling pound check. Margaret noticed Charles Berkley had made it payable to Mr. and Mrs. Benjamin Berkley and had signed it himself.

"When did he give you that?" she asked.

"At the door, under your nose. Always watch out for my father's tricks. He is very smart but discreet."

"How can we thank him?"

Benjamin shook his head. "Don't. That's why he used his little comedy. Just love him the way he is."

For a while they remained silent, then someone knocked at the door. Benjamin opened it and Judith, Margarita, Mrs. Berkley and Mrs. Timer entered the room. Mrs. Berkley gestured Benjamin to leave. "Meet us in three hours on the way to the Padre's altar."

"OK, Mom," he replied. Benjamin joined his father, Jonathan, Fred, Serge and Pepe. They were laughing as he entered the right wing. Certainly, he thought, Jonathan must be joking again.

Pepe poured him a glass of champagne. "Just for the introduction."

Everyone laughed again, and they decided to make a last inspection, suggesting, discussing, and altering previous arrangements when necessary. An hour later, they decided it was time to get dressed.

The guests were waiting when the groom, accompanied by the men-in-waiting walked out. He was dressed in a black crossed Tergal suit, a white silk shirt, and an acra-red bow tie and pocket scarf. Instantly, everyone whistled.

At the sight of the bride, when the doors of the left wing opened, the crowd feverishly applauded. A white veil covered Margaret's face. Her wedding gown was embroidered with authentic white Chinese pearls. The guests applauded, again and again.

As Fred began playing the nuptial march, motorists from the nearby highway pulled over to watch the ceremony. Even the vicar, who had witnessed the birth of Benjamin, lost his concentration during his speech. The ceremony lasted ten minutes before the exchange of vows and rings. As the couple kissed before the altar, the applause of the guests and the uninvited public echoed in the surrounding valley.

Benjamin led Margaret to their seats where the guests filed by to congratulate them and present their gifts. Serge organized a cart to tow away the gifts as they piled up. Along with parcels sent through the mail, Serge counted 495 gifts of all sizes. Finally, the chamber was half full before Serge locked it.

Fred masterfully conducted the celebration. Drinks and food abounded. The hosts and their guests danced, ate and drank until dawn. At six in the morning, the last guest left.

Benjamin brought together his father, Fred, Pepe, Serge, Jonathan and the women. He thanked them over a toast of champagne and a roasted lamb. He looked about. There was nothing else to do. The last guests had voluntarily helped in parking and cleaning.

Pepe and Margarita offered to take the group in their mini-van to the airport early in the evening. Jonathan and Judith left a short time afterward, promising to meet Benjamin and Margaret in Paris before their departure to Hawaii. After hugs and kisses, the other members of the group dispersed to their respective rooms for a much-needed nap.

In early evening, Pepe, Margarita, and the Timers accompanied the Berkley family to the airport. After farewells, Benjamin and Margaret boarded the Alitalia flight to Venice via Rome. During their honeymoon, they visited Venice, Paris, Amsterdam and spent a week in each city.

Chapter

9

A year after their wedding, Margaret graduated from the University with honors. She joined the Barclays Bank and a year later became a manager. She and Benjamin decided to have a child. Benjamin wanted only one, but Margaret wanted two or three. She argued that children would make the home more lively. With convincing arguments and examples, Benjamin, month after month, patiently pressed her into agreeing with his position.

But nature decided otherwise, and during Margaret's fourth month of pregnancy the doctor had a long talk with Margaret.

That evening she planned how to announce the news. When Benjamin came home from work, she welcomed him with a broad smile, helped him dispose of his attache case, then prepared a perfumed bath for him. During the candlelight dinner, she served chicken, peas, fries and red wine.

At first, Benjamin responded to her smiles, but he soon became embarrassed by so much attention. Even though her smile disarmed him, the sparks from her eyes tantalized him. Finally Benjamin blurted, "Twenty minutes of steady smiling tells me you have bad news for me and good news for you. In all cases, the result will be good. Can you give me a hint?"

" I'm pregnant."

"No fair. I've known that for four months or so."

"Do you want coffee, tea or fruits?"

Benjamin shot an imaginary gun at his head. "You're killing me, Love! Out with it!"

"First, come and sit on the sofa."

"Baby, what's wrong?" he asked as he docilely followed her to the couch.

"Darling, lie down and hold your breath."

She looked into his eyes and asked, "Are you sure you're ready? Can I say it now?"

He nodded then shouted desperately, "Yes. Before you turn my hair white."

"Well I... No, I mean, we, are expecting ... triplets!" she shouted victoriously.

Pretending to be in pain and disappointed, Benjamin held his forehead and lifted one arm. "And I thought it was only the Loch Ness Monster. Much worse. Oh no, my God!"

Before Margaret could comfort him, he lifted and embraced her. Finally, he let her down and said, "Oh, I got you this time. Honestly, I'm happy. I shall love to have evenings like this one more often."

"Even if they mean triplets each time?!"

"Yes! I mean no! Oh, woman, you've rattled me."

Margaret pinched and kissed him. She was grateful to be married to a man so positive.

#

Over the years, their relationship bloomed, and their love grew stronger. The prestige of Benjamin's function and his reputation raised his family's life to that of the elite of London.

Fourteen years passed and the triplets, Vanessa, Valery and Victoria were now beautiful adolescents-- but terrors. From Marylebone Road across their neighborhood to Totteham Court Road, they were known for their tricks and gags.

A conference for jurists from Commonwealth countries gave Benjamin the opportunity to send the girls to Sydney. At first, Margaret was relieved.

When the girls asked her to come with them, she refused and explained that she needed to accompany their father. Jokingly, and to exasperate her, they said, "Well, this is an occasion to have Australian boyfriends. Don't be worried if next year, you have three babies."

Margaret sometimes wondered what her life would have been like if the triplets were boys. These days, the girls were defiant and really naughty. Often, Benjamin had to discipline the girls and impose rules such as the prohibition of cigarettes, priority on school assignments, dress codes, and curfews. In spite of this, the girls managed to bypass the rules even in defiance of punishments.

The night before their departure, Margaret could not sleep. She woke Benjamin and shared her fears about leaving the girls alone for the first time in Sydney.

"Don't worry, Daddy will handle these mice. Believe me, he is a wise cat."

Margaret was not reassured. At 11 p.m. she decided to talk to the girls. Benjamin wanted to accompany her but she refused. Sometimes his masculine voice creates rebellion and stubbornness, she thought. Margaret entered the girls' room and closed the door.

The three slouched together in Valery's bed, chatting. When they saw their mother awake so late, Victoria asked, "Hey, Mom, where is your boyfriend?"

"Come under our blanket. It's warm here," Vanessa

said.

"Tell us. Is something wrong?" Valery added.

Ignoring the questions, Margaret wept. The girls looked at one another with wide eyes. Upon questioning their mother, Margaret revealed her fear of seeing them pregnant so young. Their journey to Australia was a nightmare. Compassionately, the girls put their arms around her neck and kissed her. "Mom, it was a joke. We swear to be good girls," they said.

Benjamin who was behind the door opened it, entered, lifted Margaret in his arms and without a word left the girls' room. The girls were embarrassed and decided to apologize the next day.

In their room, Benjamin kept Margaret in his arms and comforted her. She knew he was her companion, lover and best friend. Finally when she slept, she dreamt of her childhood. She was now comforted in the arms of a small African boy, after being spanked by her mother. Again, she cried in her sleep. Benjamin turned on the lights, woke her and brought her a cup of milk. He was tired but made an all-out effort to calm her. She thanked him and slept again.

Margaret and Benjamin were awake when the girls knocked at their door the next morning. Margaret had just finished telling him of her frequent dream. Benjamin knew the story in her dream as she often spoke of it. He wondered why this image of her past remained vivid. He said, "I know Gold Coast is now Ghana. Accra, the capital, has changed since independence was proclaimed, but I really wish you could meet this friend of yours and realize that he is no more the boy of your dream but a man. Anyway, let's see what can be done when we get there."

At that instant, the girls entered the room, kissed their parents and apologized. Margaret knew they were sincerely sorry and hugged them. Benjamin seized the occasion to complain. "Tell them not to call me your boyfriend anymore but politely your husband or daddy."

Benjamin threw a pillow at them and invited them for a fight. The girls jumped at the occasion and attacked their dad. As they overpowered him, Margaret came to his defense. The activity was both a 15-minute exercise and a detente.

Finally, Benjamin asked for grace. Everyone laughed, and the girls took off victorious and happy.

Chapter
10

ACCRA, GHANA 1986.

The plane landed after six hours delay in Banjul due to unfavorable weather conditions. It was just an hour before the official inauguration of the conference by the Head of State. A black official Mercedes Benz 190 with chauffeur was left at the disposition of Benjamin and his wife.

As the chauffeur drove through the main artery of the town, Margaret noticed several new buildings and houses. The billboards on the first circle did not mean anything to her but as they passed the gates of the military hospital on the right, she remembered the white wall and its black bar fences. She held Benjamin's hand. "Our residence was behind these walls. Somewhere in between lies the military hospital and the Flagstaff house."

The driver indicated that the Flagstaff house was ahead and three minutes later they passed it. Margaret pressed Benjamin's hand. "I'm sure it is behind."

"All right, the driver will drop me at the conference and leave the luggage at the hotel. Then you can make an excursion to satisfy yourself. Be very careful. Is it

Ok, Sir? What is your name?"

"Yes, Sir. My name is Koffi Bonssu," the driver replied.

"Thank you," Margaret said and kissed Benjamin.

The driver returned with Margaret and turned into a driveway leading to the first gate after the Flagstaff camp. The driver stopped the car at a respectable distance from a sentry at the gate. Armed with an automatic gun, the soldier approached as Margaret descended from the car. Politely, she asked his permission to visit the residences where she once lived.

The soldier was young and when she mentioned Gold Coast, he looked amused. He called his superior, a sergeant, who sent for a young officer. The only word she understood from their conversation was "colo" meaning colonial.

Suspicious at first, the officer presented himself as First Lieutenant Adjey. Margaret repeated the reason for visiting the residence and gave details such as the broadcasting house and the name Geo. Lieutenant Adjey looked Margaret up and down, and said the name Jacques Geo was familiar to him. He ordered the curious soldier to accompany her and indicated the closed gate on the right.

Margaret counted the first two houses then asked the driver to stop behind the third. A gate on which hung a signboard marked "Private Property--Do Not Enter" blocked the entrance. Margaret got out of the car, followed by the soldier.

"On this property lives an officer who I understand is in Germany for some months," he said.

Margaret asked to get in. "This is where I played as a child. See, there is a tree under which we sat. I would like to show you the nail we hammered into it."

The soldier was hesitant but curious. The driver started to say something but Margaret ignored him and began investigating. the property. She walked 200 meters. Behind the house, she saw a tree studded with nails.. Her heart bounced. Drawing closer, she counted 31 nails. It must be the tree.

Margaret took a card from her bag and wrote a note which she tried to affix to one nail jutting out a bit. But the breeze blew it off. In a flash of inspiration, she took out her metal nail file, pulled off one shoe and roughly engraved: Margaret Reevers Aug. 86. By the time she finished, the bottom of her shoe was scarred and the letters on the tree wobbled like those of a kindergart-ner--but she felt good.

She noticed the soldier eyeing her as though she were crazy. Margaret wanted to leave a message with him but he told her that his unit was leaving the next day. As they returned to the car, she pointed to an old house. "This is where we once lived--before independence."

The soldier nodded his head. She wondered if he were at all interested in this little bit of history that had occurred before his birth. When they arrived back at the gate, Margaret thanked the officer and the soldier. She gave him her name and her hotel address, asking, "If you could find out the name of the person living on that property, would you let me know?"

When the conference had ended and she had not received a phone call and neither had the officer shown up in person, Margaret felt disappointed.

Not until aboard their return flight did she sum up her visit to Benjamin. His thoughts still on the report he wanted to submit early next Monday, Benjamin listened passively.

Margaret took his hand in hers. "Ben, I am coming here next year, even if I only stay for a day."

"Yes, you are," he replied.

Still holding his hand, she looked at him so intently that he repeated, "Honey, I heard you. Yes, you are coming here next year."

Satisfied, she withdrew her hand and kissed him.

The following year, after many unfruitful calls to the British High Commission for information on Jacques Geo, Margaret, alone, made the trip to Accra. She planned a five-day stay but after a visit to the tree where she found an additional nail and the inscription Capt. Jacques Geo Jan. 7/87, she called home and told Benjamin she was returning the next day. She nearly missed the fully booked flight home but a no-show family saved her. She planned to return to Accra in January 1988.

With patience and understanding, Benjamin tried to calm her growing obsession for spending so much money and time to see a childhood friend. He confided his exasperation to Fred. But he understood all too well that Margaret wanted to make her dream come alive. He understood also that her quest could be one of the vulnerable stages women in their 40s sometimes went through in an unconscious desire to recapture youth.. "I love her, and do not want to lose her," he told Fred.

"Keep an eye on her, Buddy."

"How? I cannot go with her."

"Stop her then."

"Ridiculous."

Fred shrugged and frowned. "Well, let her go but with a bodyguard or send along a private eye."

None of his solutions appealed to Benjamin so once again, on January 6, 1988, Benjamin, the triplets, Valery, Vanessa and Victoria accompanied Margaret to the airport. Margaret thought the girls looked sad, and she said, hugging them one by one, "For a month at least you've teased me about tracing my roots or searching for hidden treasure, so make the best of my absence."

Benjamin's sadness was tinged with anger. Although this was apparent in both his eyes and the cold kiss he gave her, Margaret chose to ignore it at this late date.

After Margaret's flight was called, Benjamin returned each of the triplet's hugs knowing they sensed his discomfiture at Margaret's trip but helpless to overcome his feelings.

During the flight Margaret thought of her family. The girls were turning into women, more responsible and less wild. They wanted to be doctors. Their school grades were generally satisfactory. Benjamin had added some weight but was still loving and elegant. He was the only man she had known intimately and she still had no complaint. His friendliness and fidelity were unquestionable.

She knew they could depend on each other. But in some ways, he was more dependent on her and at times she felt suffocated. She was the center of gravity for the family. She would sometimes complain about being the mother of everyone including Benjamin. She laughed and questioned herself mentally. Are these not my dreams? A wonderful husband, beautiful kids, a house and a stable job. Why am I complaining? What more do I want?"

The plane landed abruptly ending her meditation. She passed through passport and custom formalities, then rented a car for five days and drove to the hotel. After a bath, she went to the reception and inquired about the restaurant.

In the restaurant, she ordered an aperitif then a meal: kenkey, a local corn farina boiled into paste with fried fish and black pepper. The waiter seemed amused when she ordered the black pepper.

As she ate, she noticed him glancing over his shoulders now and then to see the reaction to the pepper on her face. After so many years of abstinence, she had to admit the pepper was hotter than she remembered. Cautiously, she dipped the tip of the paste in it and ate more fish.

While she chewed her food, the taste of salt and dry corn leaves revived memories of her childhood with the maid whose name she could not remember. The word Adjey in her mind obscured all reconciliation. After several mental efforts, she decided to abandon it and go to bed.

Back in her room, she displayed the dresses she wanted to wear. During the day, the sky sometimes clouded over causing the weather to turn chilly. She decided to wear a green olive vest and a skirt, a crocodile leather belt and a pair of shoes in assorted colors.. Then she arranged the other clothes in the wardrobe. Later, she studied a map of the city noting places of interest. Finally, she yawned, switched off the light and slept.

Chapter

11

The next day at 7 a.m., Margaret woke up, took a shower, dressed and drove to the private property. At the gate, she had to convince an officer to let her in. The officer eyed her several times. After a desperate plea, he let her pass. She drove to the rear, far behind the trees just beside fallen bricks of what seemed to be the maids' quarters.

There, she sat in the car, observing the surroundings for features that jogged her memory. Her gaze traveled to the barbed wire fences which sagged in places. Next she noted the concrete pillars that stood proudly against the erosion of time. She listened to the radio; the news at eight, music afterward, then the news at nine. She turned off the radio and observed an eclectic montage of birds flitting overhead, either chasing one another or winged insects. Close by, an endless ballet of vultures and crows swooped and glided in the sky.

Suddenly, she heard the roar of a car's engine. Her heart raced, then pounded faster and faster. A car appeared and as it drew close she identified it as a blue BMW. A tall man of noble gait emerged. He bounded toward the tree, a hammer clasped in his left hand, a glove covering his clenched right hand. After appraising the line of nails in the tree, he held another nail to the bark and began tapping on it.

For a few moments Margaret could not move; she was so shocked to watch her dream come alive. The next thing she knew, she had jumped out of the car and was shouting. "Jacques, it's me, Margaret."

The figure stiffened then dropped the hammer and stammered her name. "Margaret? I can't believe it! My Margaret?"

They ran into each other's arms, hugging tight. Margaret cried and tears filled Jacques eyes. Silently he took her hand, and together they finished hammering the nail into the tree. Two doves in a nest above flew into the air, their wings shattering the stillness.

Margaret stepped backward, stared at him. "You are still a handsome boy; you look very young."

"And you have turned into a beautiful lady," he replied.

Before he could say more, Margaret kissed him lightly on the lips. Jacques embraced her. Pulling him to her car, Margaret opened it and from her bag, presented a package. "Happy birthday with all my love from our memorable childhood," she said and kissed him once again.

Inside the package Jacques found a small rectangular box containing a golden watch with three diamond stones encrusted on the twelve digit. Jacques thanked and kissed her. "How long are you staying?"

"Until Sunday."

"Will you kindly be my guest so that I can show you this hidden paradise? I do not know what has been your lifestyle but I can assure you that you are going to make a discovery. May I invite you for lunch?"

"With pleasure."

"I know a restaurant that serves fresh seafood, exotic and tropical fruits and drinks accompanied by music of this--of your birth country."

"I see a lot of fun ahead Jacques, but first, let us go to the hotel. I want to change my clothes for something light."

"Lead the way. I shall join you after closing the gate."

While Jacques waited in the lobby of the hotel, Margaret quickly changed and returned dressed in a blue cotton skirt opened wide at the calf. A rainbow--print shirt tied above her navel exposed her slim waist. Her tastefully exhibited bust aroused gazes among men. A set of ivory ear rings, chain and bracelets dignified her beauty.

Margaret entered Jacques' car. As they drove through the city, he pointed out the independence square, the presidential palace, a castle inherited from the British, and a neighborhood of fishermen called Labadi.

Margaret loved the restaurant immediately. The building was submerged in coconut trees whose leaves created a permanent shade and a temperate climate. The front garden of hibiscus, geranium, lily, fern and other plants perfumed the entrance. From the parking, paths of white shells bounded by rocks covered with caustic lime led to the restaurant. The structure itself was a wide hut supported by large timber logs.

Margaret and Jacques chose the terrace facing the sea. The restaurant overhung a beach of about 300 meters in width and several kilometers in length. The tables and chairs were spaciously arranged in the restaurant and covered with umbrellas. Hanging loudspeakers distilled instrumental music.

From her seat, Margaret saw the movement of white stripes of foam as the small waves of the sea splashed forward then backward. Life moved at a very slow pace here. That gave Margaret the sensation she was making a trip to a dreamland. Jacques silently watched her, while with eyes closed, she inhaled the pure and fresh air. When Margaret opened her eyes, Jacques smiled.

"Thank you for this beautiful day in my life," she

said.

A waiter appeared and they ordered vegetable salad, lobster and shrimps, wine and local fruits. Jacques suggested that they eat with their fingers, which was practical. After tasting the delicious food, they engaged in lengthy conversation.

"Margaret, what have you done for the past 30 years?" Jacques leaned toward her. "And why are you here today?"

She cut her eyes at him, smiled and replied, "Oh, it is a long story. You see, ever since we left here, there has been in almost every one of my night dreams, a little African boy consoling me. Yet, I am married to a wonderful man for 20 years with whom I had triplets-- three wonderful girls. I can't tell why this part of my childhood is unforgettable. Deep in me, I know I loved this boy and as he sits before me, handsome, young and strong, I still do. Don't ask me why. I know I have everything a woman could dream of, but ..."

She took a piece of shrimp and dipped it into Jacques' mouth. She continued narrating her life about her marriage to Benjamin Berkley; his profession, their children, the pets, the in-laws, her mother and Jonathan Jones. Jacques interrupted only with laughter at her funny anecdotes.

Four hours later, they moved beneath the coconut

trees at the edge of the beach to more comfortable arm-chairs. There, for two hours they continued their conversation. Finally, Margaret asked, "Jacques, this question has been bothering me for the past two years. The tree nails. Why have you been faithful to a promise since childhood? What have you been doing all these years?"

Jacques excused himself, waved a waiter over and ordered two full water melons with two cocktails of fresh and exotic juices. Margaret raised her eyebrows when she saw the melons but Jacques reassured her. "The best digestive I know, and basically water. Trust me, this is nothing, even to a child."

Margaret sipped her glass. "Delicious!"

Jacques nodded and began his story. "The day following the one when you and your parent left this country, I woke up, and as usual sat under the tree waiting for you. Aida, the maid, came by to inform me that you were gone forever. I cried bitterly, and told her that you promised to come and hammer the nail in that tree on my birthdays. So at the beginning, she made it a yearly ritual. Until I was 15, I scrupulously observed it. Three years later, I began to demystify this ritual. Then came the sudden death of my parents in a car accident just when I joined the Military Academy. Having nothing to turn to, I fell back to this ritual that commemorated the only wish I desired --to meet a childhood friend. I kept this folly to myself.

. "Besides, she was the only girl I ever held in my arms until she fell asleep. It may have seemed an ordeal of an hour or two to my small arms, but I did it with pure love. I am now a retired Air Force Commander, discharged for medical reasons."

Tears streaming from her eyes, Margaret stretched above the table and kissed him while a gentle breeze from the sea covered their faces with her hair. It was dusk and the sun crossed the plantation of trees to Margaret and Jacques. It reflected on zinc roofs of houses far behind and painted the sea the color of ripened orange juice.

Margaret removed her skirt, walked into the water, and collected shells while Jacques, thoughtful, watched her. When she returned, he rose, settled the check, and led her to the car. "Let me take you to the hotel so that you may rest, and if you wish, we could have dinner on the top floor. A very good band plays there."

"An hour and a half is convenient."

They drove in silence with Margaret watching scenes of people boarding trucks, buses or walking. They seemed vaguely familiar, as though seen again through a five-year-old Margaret's eyes.

For the second time in minutes, Jacques noticed a car following them but calmly continued to drive. At the hotel, he led Margaret to the elevator and ran to the entrance where he saw a European bending down and looking through a camera at the BMW. Jacques dashed over and grabbed the man by his lapels and jerked him to the top of his car. The stranger's face whitened and he began blustering.

"A detective ... or a spy? Do I have to report your presence to my colleagues of the Government? We soldiers hate spies. My name is Commander Jacques Geo."

"Detective Charles Courtney," he wheezed. "Please let me down."

"Working for?" Jacques loosened his hold and the man slid down until he was even with his captor.

"Mr. Benjamin Berkley." He stealthily held the camera behind him while rubbing at his full mustache.

Jacques stared at the brawny man. "Oh, ho. I understand. With a wonderful wife like Margaret, perhaps I may have acted likewise to salvage a marriage. But please assure Berkley that, as far as I am concerned, ours is a friendly encounter and nothing more--in spite of the film you have in that camera behind your back."

Jacques made sure the detective had driven away in his own car before Jacques got into his BMW.

When he returned, Margaret was entering the hotel from the other wing of the lobby. Jacques looked at his watch as he walked to meet her.

Margaret said, "Good evening, Jacques. You're not late. I was ready earlier and visited the surroundings. I noted a mini-zoo of birds and monkeys, a nice public garden and a large swimming pool."

Jacques embraced her, and whispered into her ear. "I thought I was your tour guide. I wanted to surprise you this night. I may resign!".

"Oh no, you don't, bad boy. You planned to take me to the park at night and I shan't let you renege."

"Me? Go back on my word? Never!".

Margaret held his arm and pulled him into the crowded bar beside the lobby. The clicks of glasses sounded here and there. Before they reached the bartender, a couple passed Margaret and greeted Jacques. Another stopped shortly after, greeted both Jacques and Margaret, and announced they were heading to the restaurant. Finally when the two old friends reached the counter, the bartender himself greeted them loudly.

"Hello, Commander!"

"My but you seem to be very popular here!" Margaret said.

"Less now." Jacques winked at her.

He ordered a whiskey and she ordered a Martini. They talked and drank for awhile but made their way out of the bar as the cloud of smoke from cigarettes thickened. Jacques coughed as they walked into the night air. Margaret seized the opportunity to tease him again. "Hey, boy, are your lungs softer than mine?"

For response, Jacques embraced her and led her to the elevator. When the elevator door opened on the top floor, Jacques, Margaret and other occupants were laughing from the jokes told between floor. Margaret laughed until she could no longer catch her breath.

Jacques held her arm up to the barricade. Looking beyond, she saw Accra by night. The city was ablaze with dots of lights. Margaret didn't remember it as being beautiful--but it was.

As they walked from one side of the walkway to another, Jacques showed her the neighborhoods and locations. They chose a table on the southern side that overlooked the most spectacular part of the city. When a waiter arrived, Margaret pulled him down and whispered her order in his ear. He left before Jacques gave his order.

Amused she said, "Just wait and you will see."

"I am very curious."

"Wait and see," replied Margaret.

Later, the waiter returned with a tray of Akplen, a paste of boiled cassava farina mixed with fermented corn farina accompanied with Okra soup with crabs. Jacques was surprised and alarmed. He asked, "Can you eat that?"

"To be sure. The last time I ate this was at the University. A friend from Togo prepared it for us. We were nine girls, and six including myself were African Europeans. Because the occasion isn't proper, I cannot demonstrate the fingers technique."

Jacques ordered the same thing and the waiter smiled in agreement before walking away. The news spread among the staff and the restaurant manager offered them free drinks.

From instrumental melodies, the band switched to songs in vogue. One by one, couples strolled to the dance floor and swung to the rhythm of each successive song. Jacques ordered a digestive drink and later invited Margaret to dance. Margaret fell immediately into the tempo so Jacques quickened his steps to the tune of the music. It was a re-composed Highlife of Jerry Hansen. Jacques kissed her forehead.

"Are you surprised?" she asked.

"No, you just confirmed my theory that from a

woman's way of walking, I can discern a gifted dancer from a trained dancer. The movements are natural and supple in the former."

"So, what am I?"

"The best I know," he replied softly.

"Flattering."

"A just compliment."

By midnight, they had danced to everything: Pop, Disco, Funk, Reggae, Highlife, Juju music and Calypso. The singer, by request, announced the last two songs. Jacques proposed to Margaret that they leave for the elevator before the rush.

"Very wise, old owl," she said tipsy from the evening.

On their way out, they thanked the manager, who invited them for the next evening, and left. The elevator stopped on the fourth floor. Only Margaret and Jacques got out. As they reached the door, Jacques said, "I truly enjoyed this--"

She held his arm and interrupted, "Jacques, I have known only Benjamin, but...."

Jacques kissed her lips punctuating her sentence.

"And you have always been faithful to your husband. You are an honorable woman and ... I love you."

Kissing him back, she pressed against him several times. "I know. I love you, too. Good night."

Without looking back, she rushed to her door, opened it, entered and closed it. For a long moment, Jacques stood where he was, then he followed her steps. He knocked once lightly at her door and Margaret opened it. She could not contain her tears over her painful dilemma which seemed a torture. Jacques held her cheeks with both hands. "Don't cry. Please don't cry."

The vein of her neck swelled and pulsated while her tear-reddened eyes implored him. Jacques looked into them and joined his lips to Margaret's lips whereupon the sensations of her body electrified him. Gently, he pressed his face against hers, forehead against forehead, then cheek against cheek, while his skin absorbed the cascading tears. They tasted each others lips. Like tentacles moving in slow motion, their tongues did battle. Unconsciously, Margaret freed Jacques from his jacket and tie, and unbuttoned his pants.

Immobilized by the fire of passion, they did not move. So pressed against each other, they knelt then lay on the carpeted floor. Margaret swirled downward to bring her dress above her waist, and reveal her very high cut panties. She pulled them aside with her fingers and Jacques penetrated her.

Margaret moaned loudly exhibiting her long held-at-bay pleasure. She shivered until reaching orgasm when she relaxed. The slow stroke of her waist and the warmth of her tight vagina propelled Jacques to his climax. And by the roar he made, she acknowledged his release. "Yes, yes, it feels so good."

Margaret interrupted the moment of silence that followed. "Jacques, somewhere in me, I desired and waited for this moment."

Although Jacques caressed her, hot tears poured out of her eyes. "Why so long? Why now?" she asked.

Jacques eluded her questions by wiping off the tears on her cheeks. "Will you have breakfast at my residence tomorrow? We could afterward make an excursion to the countryside."

Unable to say no, Margaret nodded while her hand caressed his chest. Indeed, she wanted to enjoy every minute of the present. But Jacques rose, dressed and told her he had to leave. Walking him to the door, Margaret ardently kissed him before closing the door behind him. Later, she undressed and luxuriated in a long, warm bath.

After her bath, dressed in a nightgown, she sat on her bed and felt an abrupt devouring loneliness. The room felt stifling so she slid open the glass doors of the balcony. As she looked beyond the garden, shadows of trees moved in a bizarre dance while bats shrieked around them. Margaret inhaled a lung full of air, then returned to her bed, and released it bit by bit.

She switched off the light. In the dark, while she lay on her bed, her thoughts wandered. What is Benjamin doing? Stupid question, he must be sleeping. Are the girls giving him a hard time? He said very little over the phone today when I called before leaving for the restaurant.

Must something be wrong, Margaret? she asked herself as she remembered the day she spent with Jacques, she questioned. Am I still attractive or just a curiosity? People turned as we walked but were those glares or just looks? Am I beautiful?

She tried to move but her body would not respond. It was as if she were sedated and diffusing into emptiness. Senselessly, water lapped around her from a clear and calm blue sea. She found herself floating above and staring down into the ocean depth. You are tired, Margaret, she told herself inwardly, the words echoing repeatedly in her mind. She fell deeply asleep.

Chapter

12

The next day, Margaret was awakened by songs of birds and the grating of their claws on the aluminum barricade on the balcony. The door was open and the flock, divided in three groups along the bar, chirped one after the other. From time to time, a bird in a group hung over it, flapped its wings as if it were encouraging the group. Under the sheet with her head out, Margaret watched wide-eyed. Two birds entered the room, circled and bailed out. Margaret rose to close the sliding door and the frightened flock of birds flew away. She smiled. "What an orchestra--and just for me."

Margaret walked to the bathroom, brushed her teeth, and took a shower. Later, she stood before the wardrobe, hesitated between a blue skirt and khaki pants. Finally, speaking to herself, she said aloud, "Breakfast, then excursion to the countryside. Mosquitoes? Maybe. Flies? Surely. Let's go for the khaki pants."

She took a large handbag of the same color, then decided to take a swimming suit and body lotion. She wore a white cotton shirt with shoulder straps, white socks and canvas shoes. Her makeup was light, and after several inspections, she walked to the door.

Jacques waited in the lobby, dressed in a two front-pocketed shirt, military pants and boots. He kissed Margaret. "Good morning, pretty girl. Are you going on a safari?"

"Don't I look it?" She embraced him while they walked to the car.

"We may get back late, so I hope you have everything you need."

"Everything but the birds that visited my room this morning. They couldn't stay. But I suppose we'll meet up with others?"

"With your luck, I'm certain of it." Jacques' house stood in the center of a garden. And like all Spanish architecturally designed homes, it had crispy white walls, wooden beams on the ceiling and a roof of red corrugated tiles. The floor was entirely paved with varnished red bricks. Green plants, arbitrarily arranged, gave the impression of a tranquil forest. Margaret visited each room, nodding in appreciation of this singular style. But at the sight of a photograph, she said with surprise, "Hey, Jacques! This is my..."

"That it is not. You have green eyes, and the lady in the photograph has dark brown ones. That you look somewhat alike is a coincidence, but in the photograph you can see that she is of my height while you are shorter. She is Jamaican and working as a doctor in Germany. We met 10 years ago."

Margaret examined the picture once again. "Benjamin is perfect, but I envy this woman. I wish to be in her shoes."

Jacques pulled Margaret to him and kissed her. Margaret closed her eyes and responded with a kiss. They danced to his bedroom and undressed. "I want you," she whispered.

"You've got me, lady."

As she lay on the bed and he lay on her, Margaret crossed her legs around Jacques' waist. Jacques penetrated fully while she gushed with pleasure. "I like this; it feels good."

"Then, take it."

Surprised by her boldness, Margaret opened her eyes but Jacques responded by rapid strokes of his waist. Encouraged by her lover's attitude, she ventured into erotic postures. Now she wanted to release the myriad of sexual fantasies in her. As if hypnotized, she felt waves of endless sensation overwhelming her. After ecstacy upon ecstacy, she was halted by a vertigo. "I need sustenance," she said in a child's soft voice.

Jacques remembered that tone of voice. It cut him to the quick. His Maggie's voice. Breathless after being satisfied for the third time, he caressed her face while he lay at her side. "I suppose I must feed you then."

He sighed. "Let's rinse ourselves and have breakfast."

After Jacques set the table on the terrace, he invited Margaret to the table. "Self service. And here is a cocktail of fruit juice you can mix with rum."

Margaret was impressed by the variety of mangoes, papayas and bananas on the table. Each type differed different in size and taste. "I received these fruits from a friend who is a botanist. The sweetness is less pronounced in those fruits out of season."

"How can I know the difference? These fruits are so delicious that I would content myself with them every day of my life--if I could."

"Life is very short. Better to enjoy a short savoring time than wait for abundance." Jacques' voice sounded sad to Margaret and his eyes lost their lustre for a moment..

"Philosophical? Am I listening to a wise man?"

He nodded solemnly. "I am forced to be one sometimes. I shall take some fruits, water and beer to the jeep in the garage. I hope you have not forgotten anything in the other car."

"I hope not either!"

After washing her hands, she joined him in the parking lot and admired the spacious garden. "Still, you don't have many flowers."

"Right on.. Flowers need that personal touch and I am absent for more than half of the year. I have chosen plants that do not need frequent attention."

When she jumped into the jeep, Jacques said, "We are heading toward the Aburi mountains and the neighboring town of Koforidua. Some friends will meet us at a waterfall on the mountain. Beware, they are sympathetic but extravagant in humor. Our host Peter Boateng and his wife, Rita, are longtime friends. Both are botanists, and Rita is Swedish and a linguist. She told me this morning that Peter and two friends were out deer hunting."

A few hours later, Jacques stopped at a meadow filled with blue flowers. Here, Margaret smeared herself with the tanning lotion, and stretched out on a blanket under the sun while she ate the fruits. After two hours, the basket was empty. Shyly, she said, "Jacques, I am ashamed. I have never eaten this way before. It is the first time."

"Wait until we get to the waterfall and you will see that this is nothing. But is it not a pleasure to know that it's the first time?" He winked.

Seconds passed before Margaret discerned his subtle

message and gave him a blow on the shoulder. "You are lovely," she said.

"Hey, then why hit me if I am lovely?"

"Because..." She kissed his shoulder.

Soon, they arrived at the waterfall. Jacques parked and they jumped out of the jeep. Hand in hand, they crossed to the other side of the road. They leaned over a barricade, viewed the valley far below and the green forest. A flock of vultures circled over their heads. A curious one detached itself from the group and descended to their level, approaching at every turn. Jacques quizzed, "It looks like the former president of a western European country. Who is he?" Both shouted and laughed. "Valery Giscard. Estaing of France."

For the month of January, the weather was exceptionally hot and humid. Margaret pulled Jacques across the street to the waterfall. She dipped her hand into the river. "The water is warm and clear. I would like to swim in it. Where can I undress?"

Jacques led her to the car, took a towel and said, "Put this around you while you change your shirt and khaki slacks."

He removed his boots, socks, pants and shirt. Wearing only a pair of flowery shorts, he dove into the river. The water was a little cold for him, but it was too late to get out. Margaret sauntered to the shores of the river, dove and swam to him. "Oh, wonderful!" She reached for him while he tried to escape from her hands.

Six cars drew up and created a terrible tumult with their horns. "Here they are," Jacques said as he helped Margaret out of the water to greet them.

"Peter and Rita, our hosts: Kofi and Deborah Odoteye; Dr. Alfred and Adjoa Agyemang; Professor David, alias Number 9, and Ramatu Egnonnam, and finally, Captain Charles and Susie Amoah."

One after the other, the couples jumped into the river, played and joked. Only David pretended to be ill while his wife openly contradicted him. There was laughter and screams all around to Margaret's surprise.

Just as Jacques was about to ask for her, a red Peugeot arrived its horn blasting. Jacques held Margaret's hand until the couple came out of the car. Both occupants were tall and fair in complexion but the lady was obese. She grabbed Jacques with one arm, and in a coarse voice, said, "Hello, sweety. How are you?"

She kissed Margaret's cheek while Jacques presented Margaret to them. "Mr. John and Dr. Yvonne Owusu."

John and Jacques removed their shirts, and dove

into the river.

Margaret, somewhat intimidated by the presence of all these people, waded into the water. Hands on her hips, Yvonne shouted, "I want to swim."

All the men yelled. "No!"

Then she ordered in her coarse voice. "Hey guys, dip your heads into the water or turn your eyes toward the rocks." John, for no reason, was getting out so she shouted at him. "Hey, John, you vicious pest, I say, get into the water."

John obeyed without a word. They preferred to turn their heads, and the other women, quite accustomed to the dictatorial behavior of Yvonne, laughed and clapped their hands. Yvonne shimmied from her dress and wriggled into a pair of large jean shorts and a T-shirt.

Only Professor David sat on a concrete block on the shore with his head between his knees. Yvonne snuck up to him, pushed him onto his back, and sat down heavily on his chest. The others laughed in a frenzy of excitement. Then she called, "Margaret, come here. Let me tell you a story about this boy."

Surprised, Margaret approached, and began laughing at the funny scene.

"Did you know what this boy did to me 30 years

ago?" Yvonne asked.

"Haven't a clue," Margaret replied.

"I gave him 20 invitation cards to distribute to friends and under my name this wizard added: alias Bufty Kilogram. This nickname stuck. Not only did I have to change schools several times, but I also had to become a black belt in karate and join take judo classes because of this beast. Do you know that my children went as far as Roma in Italy, to be told that their mother was nicknamed Bufty Kilogram? What should I do to him?"

Before Margaret could reply, the other women shouted, "Remove his pants."

Ramatu who knew that Yvonne would execute the request, asked Jacques to intervene. "Please stop her, Jacques."

It was partly a plea and partly a joke. Jacques called Yvonne. "Sweetheart!"

"Yes, my dear," she replied calmly..

"Please forgive him. For my sake. Because you love me."

Yvonne raised her eyebrows at Margaret who added, "Please forgive him."

Yvonne rose and said. "Number 9, why are you not in the river like everyone?"

"I am ill," David replied.

Yvonne stared at him and smiled sweetly. "Would you rather go into the river or would you rather me give you an injection of quinine."

David stripped off his clothes, jumped in the river and defiantly shouted. "Bufty!"

Everyone laughed. Margaret discovered that David teased Yvonne whenever the group met but he always evaded her torture. Yvonne swam to John, her husband, cajoled and kissed him to the applause of others. In spite of her weight, Margaret found her the most charming, enchanting person there.

By 5 p.m., everyone got out of the river. They called Peter and Rita for food. Peter went to his car and led the caravan to his house. Rita, Jacques and Margaret followed in the jeep and admired the botanical garden. From the parking lot, Yvonne ran to the gate and demanded that women should get in first.

The scent of barbecued deer meat permeated the whole house. The condiments, onions, parsley, pepper and garlic burned and wafted their odors everywhere.

Yvonne, like a matron, ordered that hands be washed, then she helped position Margaret, and protected her portion from others. "Just ask, and I shall give you everything you want," Yvonne said to Margaret who thanked her for making her feel at ease.

After the main dish, they turned to fruits. Astonished, Margaret looked at Jacques who grinned. "This is our annual orgy before everyone goes on diet."

"Except me. I am a model to a generation of fat children," Yvonne said and pounded her fist on David's head.

Ramatu complained. "Jacques, tell Yvonne to leave my husband alone. After all, he is her boss." Ramatu kissed her husband's head. "Darling, from now on, don't help her whenever she calls you at the hospital." David nodded and continued eating.

Yvonne winked at Margaret and whispered. "At the hospital, he is my boss, and sometimes, he scolds me but here I take my revenge, no?"

During a pause on the terrace, Jacques asked Yvonne for aspirin. She gave him a sharp look before handing him two tablets and a glass of water. "When are you leaving for Germany?"

"Sunday, I hope," he replied but the exchange of looks between Jacques, Yvonne and David eluded the others. Margaret caught the sad look of helplessness in the eyes of David as he tried to bow his head. Wondering what was being withheld from her, Margaret noted that Ramatu was not in the picture either.

Feeling lonely in the crowd of friends, Margaret asked to call home. Rita directed her to the bedroom for privacy. Benjamin answered when the phone rang. Everything was going on smoothly, he said, and repeated how much he loved her and missed her. "I miss and love you too. Pray for me, I shall be home on Sunday. Kiss the kids on my behalf, darling. Goodbye."

When Margaret opened the door, the others were dancing. Yvonne danced a calypso in David's arms. Margaret said, "Ah! Finished with the cat-and-mouse dispute." David winked at her.

Margaret invited Jacques to the floor. They danced until 11 p.m., then Jacques suggested returning to Accra. He invited all of them to a reception at his house in honor of Margaret on Saturday. One after the other, they kissed and hugged her. Margaret realized she really liked these friends of Jacques'. What a memorable day, she thought, I shall remember it forever.

In the car, Margaret turned to Jacques. "Jacques, sympathetic is not the right word to describe your friends. I should say that they are fraternal. Nowhere have I seen such friendliness and kindness."

SOTERO AGBOTON

"Margaret, like me, they know how short life is," Jacques replied.

They had covered a distance of 10 kilometers when Jacques noticed a car with a European occupant parked on the side of the road. Jacques reduced his speed, then recognized him. "Ha! It is our detective. His car has broken down."

Jacques braked to a halt, inspected the detective's car, and offered to tow it. Detective Courtney readily agreed and they set to work linking the two cars.

When Jacques slid back into his own front seat and started the engine, Margaret questioned him. "What is this nonsense about a detective?"

"Your husband hired him." Jacques' voice was intentionally low. Suddenly Margaret became angry. "Stop the car. I want to have a word with him. Jacques, please stop the car."

Jacques held her arm and pressed it lightly.. "Margaret, did you speak to Benjamin this evening?"

"Yes," she replied.

"Did he say he missed you?"

"Yes."

"I know that you are a wonderful woman, and if I were him, I may have acted the same way. I hope you understand what it means to be one's everything. Something far beyond physical possession or material success: love, simple and truthful. You can have a word with the detective at the hotel, but I wish thereafter, you do not remember it or refer it to Benjamin. Are you all right? Do you know what I mean?"

After a few moments of thought, she answered, "Yes, thank you."

"Any time. Now would you look in the bag behind you and pull out the two leather jackets. The air is getting cold."

Margaret did as he asked and they both felt quite warm. Restrained by the seatbelt, Margaret dozed off. Jacques drove as cautiously as he could and when the car stopped, Margaret was deeply asleep. Jacques removed the towing cord between the cars, then woke Margaret and led her to her room. He kissed her and left.

Scanning the parking lot, Jacques noted that the detective and his car were gone. So, Jacques drove home and after a bath went to bed. He woke up twice that night, first to close the windows, second to take two more blankets. He had a fever. He knew that a headache and a fever were the forerunners of his usual sickness. Thank goodness my wish has come true, he thought.

Chapter

13

At 8 a.m. on Saturday, after a bath, Margaret dressed and went down to the lobby. She walked to the reception and her eyes met those of the detective who was comfortably seated in a couch. She turned, moved in his direction and calmly asked, "May I have a word with you? My name is Margaret Berkley as you certainly know."

He looked up, pretending he'd just seen her. "But of course."

"I understand that you've been hired by my husband, which is unfortunate but you've stupidly exposed yourself in a manner which a beginner in your profession could have avoided. I wish to stress that the gentleman in my company is a dear friend from my childhood in Accra.

For your information, I shall be shopping, then driving to the beach. Early this evening, a reception will be held in my honor at my friend's residence. Afterward, I shall invite him, if he wishes to come, to my hotel room. However, the door will be open. I am giving you permission to enter and take notes or pictures of anything you feel compromises me. I take full responsibility for the consequences. I hope you are well paid for snooping. Thank you for listening to me."

The detective shook his head as if to say, Now, I've heard it all as she left for the entrance of the hotel.

Margaret took her car and drove to the nearby market. She bought some native clothes, four masks, a local drum, and a pair of leather sandals for each member of her family. After walking an hour and half, and wandering aimlessly, she returned to her car and drove back to the hotel.

Jacques had called and left a message at the desk. Margaret called but Jacques' maid said that he had gone out. She asked the maid, and later the receptionist, to inform Jacques that she was going to the beach.

Although the sea felt old at this time of the year to Africans, Europeans found it pleasant. Margaret saw dozens of tourists either swimming or tanning themselves. Excited native children ventured slowly into the water, screaming and playing while parents or adults observed under the shade of giant umbrellas or coconut trees.

Margaret smeared passion fruit lotion over her body and dived into the sea. She swam beyond the breakers, turned on her back, floated and relaxed. The ocean and blue skies calmed her. "What a wonderful world I left," she said to herself.

She pressed her chin against her chest and scanned the shores. The beach, the people, the trees, the restaurants, the house far behind; everything she saw was motionless. Yes, as she had thought earlier, here, the pace of life is slow.

Suddenly, shaken by the fear of isolation, she swam back to the shore, spread out a towel and lay on it. Now and then, Margaret switched from her back to her stomach. The weather was humid. Every 15 minutes or so, Margaret washed her body in the shower, cooling off to get hot again. She enjoyed this repeated activity. By 5 p.m., she was satisfactorily tanned so she decided to walk to the restaurant for a sandwich.

Jacques, who was sitting under the trees, waved at her. Margaret walked to him, kissed him and sat on his lap.

"How do you find me?" she asked.

"Beautiful, superb, irresistible," he replied and swallowed hard.

"Jacques, be honest," she pleaded.

"I don't like to swear, but like an Italian, I swear on my mother's tomb. Peace unto her soul. Just wait to see the reaction of your husband and children."

Satisfied, Margaret took a seat and asked. "What

can I offer you?"

"Sorry, I am the host," Jacques replied.

He called a waiter and she ordered spaghetti, then fruits while Jacques chose to eat only mangoes and drink water. When Jacques paid the check, he escorted Margaret to her car and said, "I shall pick you up at 7:30. I'm sorry to have only 60 guests. Many friends had other engagements."

"Jacques, this is a great honor, and I just can't express my gratitude." She waved at him and drove to the hotel.

At 7:30 p.m., Jacques knocked at the door. Margaret was elegantly dressed in a gold embroidered black evening gown, a white woolen shawl over her shoulders.

"No princess or queen in this world can match your beauty." Jacques kissed her hand.

When they arrived at Jacques' residence, Margaret was impressed by the display of lamps beneath plants and trees in the garden. She held Jacques' arm, stopped and asked, "Why me, Jacques?"

"Because I have lived for this day, it is the least I can do. I cannot tell you what the future holds for us."

Cars arrived one after the other and guests poured in. Margaret officiated as a principal hostess but begged Jacques not to have her deliver a speech. Waiters hired from the army executed their jobs well. Since there was no speech, the reception turned into a party. To Margaret's astonishment, many guests brought gifts to her. The Aburi group was also there. For an instant, Margaret slipped into the kitchen and called home as she did every evening.

After narrating her day's activity to Benjamin, he asked, "Are you sure this guy is not in love with you?"

"We are in love," she replied.

Benjamin's heart pounded but calmly Margaret added, "Not the way you think and can understand. Remember I love you."

Benjamin was confused when he hung up the phone.

Margaret and Jacques danced and their guests enjoyed themselves until 2 a.m. Mr. and Mrs. Owusu were among the last guests to leave. Yvonne asked Jacques, "Are you leaving the keys of your house before flying to Germany?"

"No, I may be back soon," he replied.

Yvonne hugged and held him for a long time while other guests waited to say good-bye. Her relationship with Jacques must be special, Margaret imagined although she was somehow disturbed by the passiveness of John Owusu.

Later, Jacques took Margaret to the hotel and led her to her door. Margaret held his arm. "Come in and stay with me all night, not for any reason other than to be with me. We can talk, play chess if you wish, listen to music or whatever."

"OK," he replied to stop what was ending up as a plea.

Margaret left the door slightly open. Jacques did not see the maneuver as a wall separated the corridor from the room. Margaret turned off the lights of the corridor before she walked to the bathroom and changed into a jogging outfit. Meanwhile, Jacques removed his coat and tie.

Seated at the end of the bed facing the corridor, she pulled out a low table, displaying a chess board, and invited Jacques to approach and sit in the only arm chair available. For the first two games, she defeated Jacques. From time to time, she looked over his shoulders. Once she caught a shadow projected by the light in the gallery, furtively retreating.

For the next four games, Jacques won. "I see. You tactically let me win the first two games and gave me a spanking. You're a very intelligent player."

Margaret changed her seating position several times then asked Jacques to bring the board down to the carpet. She was tired and Jacques took advantage of her mistakes. He removed his shoes to feel at ease, and finally after waiting long for his turn, he groaned and lay on his back and closed his eyes. "Call me if you are through," he said.

She looked at him, pushed the board, and in resignation said, "You are the champion. What is going to be your trophy?"

"Your friendship," he replied.

"I swear you have it."

After a minute of silence, she asked. "Jacques, why didn't you make this encounter possible 20 years ago?"

"I never made anything, Margaret. Life or God, if you believe in him, brought everything to me. Everything came, I believe, at the best time."

The best time! What is the best time? she thought and repeated aloud, "The best time!"

Her eyes were closed. She opened them and saw a shadow move backward. Poor detective, he must be disappointed, she thought.

Margaret lifted her arms and stretched them to

Jacques' head. His hair felt curly and woolly. The skin on his cheeks, eyes, mouth and chin felt soft. From his regular breathing, she knew he was sleeping so she withdrew her hands. She rose, turned and looked at him. His body was immobile and his fingers were planted in the carpet. He looks cold, she thought. She, took a blanket and covered him.

Uncomfortable on the carpet, she climbed onto the bed and closed her eyes. Two hours later, she heard the door close and saw the lights go off. From the perceptible daylight, she glimpsed a note on the desk and snatched it up. "I am going home to put your gifts in suitcases. My flight to Frankfurt is an hour after yours. I shall pick you up at noon. "It was signed simply, Jacques.

Margaret looked at her watch. It was 6 a.m., so she called the reception desk and asked for KLM's reservation. The economy and business classes were fully booked so she requested two first-class seats. After Margaret gave their names, the agent replied, "Sorry, Madam, but passenger Jacques Geo is already confirmed in first class."

"Please reserve Mrs. Margaret Berkley in the first class to Paris via Frankfurt, and if possible, seated by Mr. Jacques Geo. I have a full fare economy flight coupon to London, and I shall be paying the difference by credit card."

"You are confirmed in seat 5B with Mr. Jacques Geo," the agent said.

Margaret called London and told Benjamin of her plans to travel to Paris. She did not really asked for his consent so Benjamin acknowledged the information. At this time, an absence by Margaret for one extra day made no difference.

When Jacques arrived, Margaret stood in the lobby settling her bills. She looked at him and smiled.

"There is something you have prepared for me or you are preparing but beware, I have a weak heart and therefore cannot take surprises," Jacques said.

He looked serious and instantly, Margaret was disarmed. Was this the reason Yvonne spared him? As they walked to the car, she said in a sweet voice. "I am taking the flight with you to Paris via Frankfurt."

"Why?"

"Because that is the maximum time I can spend with you before we separate."

She was honest but sad, too. As he drove to the airport, Jacques kept glancing at Margaret and smiling.

"What's funny?" she finally asked.

"You're such an admirable woman," he replied and winked.

"Are you making fun of me?"

"Ah, if I wasn't smart and accustomed to eyes like yours, you would have taken me for a ride. By the way, the heart attack issue was a farce."

"Jacques, you wizard!" Margaret shouted.

"No, just smart. I had to know what surprise you had for me." They laughed.

At the airport, Margaret went to the ticket office for a new ticket while Jacques checked the baggage pulled by porters to the departures. Margaret joined him later, just when he was settling her excess baggage weight charges. She kissed him on the neck. After customs and immigration, they walked to the first-class lounge. Jacques continued their conversation with jokes.

When the plane took off, only Margaret forgot to fasten her seatbelt. The German steward who came to remind her, asked, "What joke have you told to cause laughter from this beautiful lady?" After the remark from the steward, Jacques remained silent but as Margaret looked at his eyes, she could not stop laughing. Jacques closed his eyes and pretended he was sleeping until Margaret cooled down.

The flight was non-stop and Margaret had just enough time to make a transfer for her last journey to Paris. Service aboard first class was excellent, but Jacques drank only water. Dinner was served, and a short time after, a film was shown. Margaret took Jacques's hand, fingers across fingers, and asked, "When will I see you again?"

He pressed her fingers and withdrawing his wallet from his pocket, gave her a card on which was embossed the address of his girlfriend, Dr. Melanie Cockrum. Margaret gave him her business card with her home phone number. "Please call me on Tuesday. I am on vacation for two weeks."

Just before the plane landed, Margaret kissed his hand and thanked him for the wonderful time. In reply, Jacques kissed her forehead. Once again, they kissed as they separated in the transfer lounge.

Margaret's flight to Paris was a short one. After passport control and baggage clearance, she hailed the first taxi headed towards downtown Paris. She was tired, and once in her hotel room, went to bed early.

The next morning, she called home. Benjamin was out, and Vanessa answered the call. Valery and Victoria wanted to talk to their mother. Each girl gave an exhaustive list of articles to buy. At the end, Margaret checked the list and asked, "Who will pay for these articles?"

Victoria answered, "Hey, Mom, you owe us that because we kept the morale of your boyfriend high, and he weighs 10 pounds more."

"What? Ten pounds in five days? What did you girls give him to eat? I had better come home."

Margaret spent the day shopping and touring Paris: the Seine River, the Eiffel Tower, and the Montparnasse Tower. She made a trip to the castle of Versailles and returned to the Champs Elysees. There, she walked around the Arc de Triomphe, made stops in cafes and nodded to sympathetic faces. At the end, she returned to the hotel very exhausted.

The receptionist handed her two slips requiring an urgent call to Mr. Benjamin Berkley. She took the elevator to her room and walked directly to the bathroom for a bath. After, she dressed then lay back against the pillows on her bed and called London. The phone rang more than eight times before Benjamin answered.

"Hello," said a broken voice.

"Can I speak to... Ben, what's wrong?"

"I want you to come home immediately," he said.

"Why? I need to make..."

He interrupted her and screamed. "Please, I say come

home!" He hung up.

Margaret dialed the reception desk and asked for the central airlines reservations, but the reservationist told her no more flights were available tonight. So she booked a 6:45 a.m. flight to London and dialed her home again. Several times, she dialed wrong numbers, then she began to tremble.

Suddenly she went blank and could not remember her phone number. She rose to take her bag, fumbled, caught her bag, withdrew a card and dialed the correct number. The phone rang several times before Benjamin replied, Before he could speak, she begged him. "Please Ben, is it Vanessa?"

"No," he replied.

"Victoria?"

"No."

"Something to do with the children?"

"No."

"Your parents?"

"No."

"My mother or Jonathan?" she screamed.

"No. Please come home. Please, please, I'm very sorry." Again he hung up.

Margaret tried to sleep but she could not. She turned on the bed several times: from her stomach to her side, to her back, and again to her stomach. She rose and called the reception desk to reserve a taxi for 5 a.m. She insisted that she wanted a reliable taxi company.

Most of the night she walked to and fro in the room. In between pacing, she packed her luggage and set it by the door.

Finally, she removed her nightgown, dressed, looked time and time again at her watch, and sat in the armchair until dawn.

Chapter
14

The plane landed on time at London's Heathrow airport. Margaret gnawed the nails on her fingers and chewed part of her boarding-pass. She dashed out of the plane as soon as she could, but a Custom officer who noticed her nervousness, stopped her for declaration. While tears fell on her cheeks, Margaret said, "Excuse me, Sir, there is something serious happening in my home. I can leave my baggage, my passport, and report later."

Impassively, the officer took her passport, looked in her bag and her purse. Taking his time, he opened the first two suitcases and a travel bag and meticulously searched them.

Margaret complained. "You have no right. This is just unfair."

Abruptly she spotted a familiar face. Fred Timer had evidently witnessed the scene because he started toward her when the Custom officer released her. Margaret wasted no time greeting Fred but ran past him and signalled to a chauffeur pushing an empty trolley. Margaret pushed the chauffeur as he pushed the cart.

Fred caught up with her and kept stride.

"Where is Ben?" she asked.

"At home, I believe," replied Fred.

"What do you mean by I believe?"

"Sorry, Margaret, he called me to come and pick you up," Fred said defensively as he helped the attendant load her luggage into his car.

After a moment of silence on the road, she asked, "What's wrong?"

"I do not know, Margaret," Fred replied.

"Oh, my God, what do you mean by you don't know, Fred?" she shouted.

The chauffeur turned to look at them but Fred shrugged and stared passively in front of him. He had met Benjamin the day before, and to Fred's knowledge, nothing was wrong. Neither spoke until they arrived home where Margaret thanked him, and hurriedly climbed the stairs. She took out her keys, opened the door and ran into the house. She dashed to her room but the door was locked. Victoria opened the door of the girls' room and Margaret questioned her. "What's wrong?"

"We don't know. You received a telegram, and since last night, Daddy locked himself in your room."

"Help Fred's chauffeur with the luggage," Margaret instructed and walked to the other door.

She pounded her fist at the door and called, "Benjamin!". After a few seconds, the door opened. Benjamin's eyes were swollen and red. Margaret knelt before him as he sat on the bed. She held his head with her two hands and tried to understand what was wrong. All she heard was, "Darling, Honey, I am deeply sorry for you."

Benjamin turned his head in the direction of the telegram that Margaret picked up. She read it and felt stunned. It announced the death of Jacques Geo and was signed by Melanie. Instantly, the blood mounted into her eyes and blurred the letters and the lines on the paper. Margaret burst into a savage and painful outcry. Vaguely she heard the girls running into the room and felt Benjamin embracing her.

Victoria, then Vanessa, and Valery, all affected by the griefs of their parents, cried. Later, Benjamin put Margaret to bed while he herded the girls out. "Please leave her alone. Your mother has lost her best friend. I know she is in deep pain."

Benjamin had taken two weeks off to spend a second honeymoon with Margaret on her return, but the tragic news foiled his plans.

A day after Benjamin left on vacation, a package from detective Charles Courtney arrived, and was dropped in a pending file by his secretary.

Margaret raged and cried for the day, the night and the following day. Sedatives from the doctor could not hold her longer than an hour. Her sorrow was profound and she had not eaten since her arrival. Her hair was shaggy and wet with tears from her swollen eyes.

Early in the morning, Benjamin undressed and lifted her to the bathroom and down into the tub. He turned on the faucet. The running water made Margaret cry. Affectionately, he washed and dried her. He brushed her hair, perfumed her body with cologne, kissed her cheek and gently led her to the bedroom. After pulling open five drawers, he found at last, one with 20 or more panties neatly arranged. What're all those for? he thought. I guess I don't have more than ten.

With difficulty, he dressed her, pulled one of his large T-shirts over her, and later asked the girls to serve them hot milk . Margaret drank two cups while he sipped his first. Then Margaret opened her eyes, and in a hoarse, almost inaudible voice said, "Call Melanie."

I did on Sunday and yesterday."

"I want to speak to her," she said in halting words.

Benjamin dialed the number and placed the receiver in Margaret's hand.

"Melanie," a soft voice answered at the other end.

"Margaret Berkley speaking." Then after a sob, she repeated, "It's Margaret. We're coming tomorrow. We love you."

"I love you, too. Good-bye," replied Melanie.

Benjamin patted her thigh, kissed her forehead, helped her into the bed. "Let me take care of packing our luggage."

Chapter

15

When the plane landed in Frankfurt, a ground hostess met the Berkleys. Evidently confused by the resemblance of the women, she said to Margaret, "Your sister, Miss Melanie Cockrum, is waiting for you in a special lounge."

Melanie sat with her back upright and her eyes toward the floor. At the door, the hostess pointed her finger at Melanie and turned away. Margaret and Benjamin walked to the woman. At the sight of her face, Benjamin pressed Margaret's shoulder. He was astonished by the incredible similarity. Melanie jumped into Margaret's arms and both wept. Benjamin wiped tears from his eyes.

The ceremony at the crematory was stirring but as Jacques had expressed in his will, everything was executed accordingly. It was a special and unusual ceremony to most mourners from Africa, especially the Aburi friends. Respectfully, they bowed to Jacques' last wish.

Late that night, Yvonne confided to the Berkleys. "You should know, Jacques' days were numbered. He suffered from leukemia and this unexpected heart attack prematurely ended what could have been an agonizing death. It is sad and disheartening, but it's the best solution."

On their flight back to London, Margaret, on many occasions, recalled the memorable moments spent with Jacques.

Three months and a half passed, when one morning Margaret awoke with full energy. She planned a busy day at home, prepared breakfast for her family, and escorted Benjamin to the door as he left for work.

"Good day with love." She kissed him.

"I love you," he replied and kissed her hard.

She locked the door, turned, then suddenly, as if dark clouds descended from nowhere, she burst into tears, and sobbed. Ten minutes afterwards, she wiped her tears, and washed dishes.

Later, as she climbed to her room, waves of nausea forced her to cling three times to the balustrade. The sickness happened two days in a row, and although Margaret took a Friday off to rest from the workload of her new post, she anguished.

Four weeks had passed since her return to work when the phone rang at Margaret's office. A bank official asked her to present herself with an attorney and a witness to discharge papers in execution of a will.

"I think it's a mistake," she said.

"Are you Margaret Reever, the wife of Lord Berkley?"

"Yes," replied Margaret.

"Then, may I ask you to be here tomorrow at 9 a.m., if convenient, with a lawyer and a witness."

"Yes," Margaret answered.

During supper, she informed Benjamin who pretended not to hear what she was saying. When they were alone in their room, he asked, "What is it about, Honey. Are any of your relatives dead?"

"My aunt but that was a long time ago. Besides her immediate relative is my mother."

"Could your parents have died without our knowledge?"

"Certainly not," she screamed and started to cry.

"Sorry. Tomorrow will tell."

The next day, they were led to the office of the bank's president. A gentleman cordially greeted and invited them to a luxurious office. With a box in one hand, and papers in the other, he said, "Please read this check and sign. We have, if you need one, safes available here and in other branches of our bank."

Margaret opened the box and found five bars of gold, each weighing approximately one and a half kilograms. Each bar represented a member of her family. She signed the paper before her and told the bank's president that they were clients of one of the branches. Benjamin added, "We already have a safe."

In the car, Margaret unsealed the envelope attached to the box and found in it a copy of the will, legalized and witnessed by the signatures of Yvonne and Rita, under which was the seal of a notary. A card was also attached. Margaret read it aloud. "Just to thank you for our golden friendship. God bless you, your wonderful husband and your daughters."

It was signed by Jacques Geo.

Margaret leaned her head on Benjamin's shoulder and cried. Benjamin silently wept as he drove the car home.

LORD BERKLEY's WIFE IS AN ADDENDUM TO THE MISTRESS OF THE FISH TRADING POST.